LEARN SMART

狄克生
片語 這樣背

DIXON'S IDIOMS

Introduction

本書使用導覽

1. 情境會話

> 將片語融合在情境會話中，幫助靈活運用。

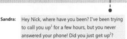

Unit 01 The School Test 學校考試

Sandra and Nick talk about their history test.
珊卓拉和尼克在討論歷史考試。

Sandra: Hey Nick, where have you been? I've been trying to call you up[1] for a few hours, but you never answered your phone! Did you just get up[2]?

Nick: No, I've been awake for a few hours now. I think I forgot to turn on[3] my cell phone this morning. Come in and take off[4] your jacket. Make yourself comfortable.

Sandra: We don't have time to chat here. Put on[5] your jacket and let's go!

Nick: Why?

Sandra: We have that big history test to study for.

Nick: I'll study for it sooner or later[6]. What's the rush?

Sandra: The test is in three hours!

Nick: Yikes! I forgot! We'd better get started right away[7]. Let me call my mom to pick us up[8] and take us to the library.

珊卓拉：　喔，尼克，你到哪去了？我打電話找你找了好幾個小時，你都沒接電話！你才睡醒床嗎？

尼克：　不，我醒來好幾個小時了。我想我早上忘記關掉。進來脫下夾克，別拘束。

珊卓拉：　我們沒時間在這裡聊天了，把

> 右頁搭配對話翻譯，有效輔助學習。

尼克：　為什麼？

珊卓拉：　我們要準備歷史大考。

尼克：　我還早會準備的，急什麼呢？

珊卓拉：　考試再過三個小時就要開始了！

尼克：　天啊！我都忘了！我們最好馬上出門。我要叫我媽來接我們，送我們到圖書館。

turn on the TV 打開電視

take off 脫下夾克

2. 片語分類

> 依使用頻率和程度編排。

> 多樣化例句，清楚示範片語用法。

1 call up　打電話給某人

- I was bored Friday night, so I **called up** some old friends and organized a party.
星期五晚上我很無聊，於打電話給幾個老朋友，籌劃同一個派對。

- Derek told the pretty girl she could **call** him **up** sometime, but she never did.
德瑞克告訴那個漂亮的女孩說她可以打電話給他，但她從未打過。

2 get up　叫醒某人；起床

- My mom **gets** me **up** every day before school.
我媽媽每天上學前會叫我起床。

- I brush my teeth twice a day: when I **get up** and before I go to bed.
我每天刷兩次牙：上床前和起床後。

3 turn on　打開（電器或設備）；突然攻擊某人

- Hey, **turn** the TV **on**, or we'll miss the game!
快，打開電視，否則我們的就要錯過比賽了！

- Frank couldn't figure out why his dinner was still cold

4 take off　脫掉（衣服、首飾）；（飛機）起飛

- When entering an official building in America, a male should **take off** his hat.
在美國，進入辦公門面的大樓時，男士一定要脫帽。

- It was cloudy out, so Jen took her sunglasses **off** and put them in her pocket.
外面天空陰沉沉的，所以珍將她的太陽眼鏡放在口袋。

5 put on　穿戴（衣服或配件）；塗抹；愚弄

- I **put on** my watch every morning before work.
我每天早上上班前會戴上手錶。

- Tim **put** his winter hat **on** before he went out to play in the snow.
提姆在出去玩雪前，把冬帽戴上。

- Is there a mirror somewhere? I need to **put** my makeup **on**.
這裡有鏡子嗎？我得補補妝。

- He's **put on** a lot of weight since he gave up smoking.
他戒煙後胖了好多。

- You didn't believe him, did you? He was just **putting** you **on**.
你沒有把他當真對吧？他只是在要你罷了。

3. 彩圖圖解

結合情境彩圖，快速加強記憶。

7 think over 仔細考慮；深思熟慮

- Jan wasn't sure if it was a good idea to buy the car, so she **thought** it **over** for a few days.
  珍不確定買車是否是個好主意，所以她仔細考慮了好幾天。

- After **thinking over** the assignment, Marion got started with her research.
  瑪莉安在認真思索過這份工作後便開始進行研究。

8 try on 試穿

- Before you buy those jeans, **try** them **on** to make sure they fit.
  買牛仔褲前，記得要試穿以便確定是否合身。

- If you don't have any nice shoes to wear with your suit, you can **try on** mine; if they fit, you can borrow them.
  你若是沒有好搭的鞋能搭套裝，可以試穿我的，如果合腳，你可以借去穿。

8 take a walk (stroll, hike, etc.) 散步；閒逛

- After a large dinner, Tracy likes to **take a stroll** around the park.
  崔西喜歡在用過豐盛的晚餐後到公園裡散步。

- Last weekend, Franz and his family went on a picnic and then **took a hike** in the nearby hills.
  法蘭斯上星期和家人去野餐，然後在附近的山區健行。

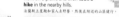

10 take a trip 遠行；旅行

- Reg won't come in to work next week because he's **taking a trip** to Chicago for a business meeting.
  雷格下星期不會來上班，因為他要到芝加哥出差開會。

- This summer, Barbra plans to **take a trip** to Mexico.
  芭芭拉計畫這個夏天到墨西哥旅行。

11 put away 收拾；收起來；儲存；大吃特吃

- James told his little sister to **put away** all her toys before their parents got home.
  詹姆斯叫妹妹在父母回家前把玩具收拾好。

- The teacher told me to **put** my cell phone **away** because I was using it during class.
  我上課時在用手機，老師要我把它收起來。

- I decided to **put away** a few dollars each week.
  我決定每個星期都要存下一點錢。

- He **put away** a whole box of chocolates in one evening.
  他一個晚上就吃掉了整盒巧克力。

12 so far 到目前為止

- My first semester at college is going well **so far**—though we haven't had any tests yet.
  我在大學的第一個學期到目前為止都很順利，儘管我們還沒考試過。

- **So far** during this car ride, we've passed three gas stations without stopping.
  到目前為止，我們已經開車經過了三間加油站，但都沒有停下來。

CONTENTS

Unit

The School Test
學校考試

Sandra and Nick talk about their history test.
珊卓拉和尼克在談論歷史考試。

Sandra:	Hey Nick, where have you been? I've been trying to **call** you **up**[1] for a few hours, but you never answered your phone! Did you just **get up**[2]?
Nick:	No, I've been awake for a few hours now. I think I forgot to **turn on**[3] my cell phone this morning. Come in and **take off**[4] your jacket. Make yourself comfortable.
Sandra:	We don't have time to chat here. **Put on**[5] your jacket and let's go!
Nick:	Why?
Sandra:	We have that big history test to study for.
Nick:	I'll study for it **sooner or later**[6]. What's the rush?
Sandra:	The test is in three hours!
Nick:	Yikes! I forgot! We'd better get started **right away**[7]. Let me call my mom to **pick** us **up**[8] and take us to the library.

珊卓拉： 嘿，尼克，你到哪去了？我**打電話**找你找了好幾個小時，你都沒接電話！你才剛**起床**嗎？

尼克： 不，我醒來好幾個小時了。我想我早上忘記**開**機了。進來**脫下**夾克，別拘束。

珊卓拉： 我們沒時間在這裡聊天了。把夾克**穿上**，我們快走吧！

尼克： 為什麼？

珊卓拉： 我們要準備歷史大考了。

尼克： 我**遲早**會準備的，急什麼呢？

珊卓拉： 考試再過三個小時就要開始了！

尼克： 天啊！我都忘了！我們最好**馬上**出門。我要叫我媽來**接**我們，送我們到圖書館。

turn on the TV 打開電視

take off 脫下

3

1   call up   打電話給某人

- I was bored Friday night, so I **called up** some old friends and organized a party.
  星期五晚上我很無聊，就打電話給幾個老朋友，籌劃開一個派對。

- Derek told the pretty girl she could **call** him **up** sometime, but she never did.
  德瑞克告訴那個漂亮女孩改天可以打電話給他，但她從未打過。

2   get up   叫醒某人；起床

- My mom **gets** me **up** every day before school.
  我媽媽每天上學前會叫我起床。

- I brush my teeth twice a day: when I **get up** and before I go to bed.
  我每天刷兩次牙：上床前和起床後。

get up 起床

3   turn on   打開（電器或設備）；突然攻擊某人

- Hey, **turn** the TV **on**, or we'll miss the game!
  嘿，打開電視，否則我們就要錯過比賽了！

- Frank couldn't figure out why his dinner was still cold until he saw that he had forgotten to **turn on** the oven.
  法蘭克想不透為何晚餐還是冷的，直到他發現忘了把烤箱打開。

- I tried to help her stand up, but she **turned on** me, shouting, "Get off!"
  我想扶她站好，但她突然吼我說：「滾開！」

4 take off 脫掉（衣鞋、首飾）；（飛機）起飛

- When entering an official building in America, a male should **take off** his hat.
  在美國，進入講究門面的大樓時，男士一定要脫帽。

- It was cloudy out, so Jen **took** her sunglasses **off** and put them in her pocket.
  外面天空陰陰的，所以珍摘下太陽眼鏡放在口袋。

5 put on 穿戴（衣服或配件）；塗抹；愚弄

- I **put on** my watch every morning before work.
  我每天早上上班前會戴上手錶。

- Tim **put** his winter hat **on** before he went out to play in the snow.
  提姆在出去玩雪前，把冬帽戴上。

put on 戴上

- Is there a mirror somewhere? I need to **put** my makeup **on**.
  這裡有鏡子嗎？我得補個妝。

- He's **put on** a lot of weight since he gave up smoking.
  他戒菸後胖了好多。

- You didn't believe him, did you? He was just **putting** you **on**. 你沒有把他當真對吧？他只是在耍你耶。

6 sooner or later 遲早；總有一天

- Jay isn't sure when he'll finish his paper, but he's convinced he'll complete it **sooner or later**.
  傑不確定何時會完成論文，但他相信他遲早會完成的。

- Life may be difficult for you now, but **sooner or later** it has to get better.
  現在生活對你來說也許很困難，但情況總有一天會好轉。

7　right away　馬上；立刻

- I have to leave **right away**; otherwise, I will be late.
  我必須馬上離開，否則會遲到。

8　pick up　拾起；購買；用汽車搭載或接送某人

- Jake **picked up** the kitten and took it to its mother.
  傑克撿起了小貓，把牠帶到媽媽的身邊。

pick up 拾起

- We can **pick up** some coffee and food on the way to the library.
  我們可以在去圖書館的路上買些咖啡和食物。

- I have to **pick up** my sister from soccer practice and drive her home.
  妹妹練完足球後我必須去接她，然後載她回家。

pick up（用汽車）接送

9　get in　上車 (汽車、計程車等小型車)；到達

- **Get in** the car, and I'll give you a ride!
  上車吧，我載你去！

get out of 下車

- Do you know what time Mark's plane **gets in**?
  你知道馬克的飛機幾點到嗎？

get on a plane 上飛機

10 get on

上車
（大型交通工具：巴士、火車、飛機、船等）

- If you don't have a ticket, you can't **get on** the train.
  如果你沒有車票，就不能上火車。

- The plane was almost full by the time I **got on**.
  我上飛機時，機上幾乎已經都坐滿人了。

get on a bus 上公車

11 at first

起初；原來；剛開始

- Although English was hard **at first**, after I had studied it for a few months, it became easier.
  雖然英語剛開始很難，但我學了幾個月後，就變得比較容易了。

- When Joan met Lou, she didn't like him **at first**; however, ten months later, they were married.
  瓊安和盧相遇時，她起初並不喜歡他，但是 10 個月後，他們結婚了。

- If **at first** you don't succeed, try and try again.
  一試不成功，就再試一次。

02

Shopping
逛街購物

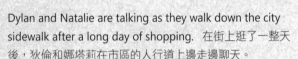

Dylan and Natalie are talking as they walk down the city sidewalk after a long day of shopping. 在街上逛了一整天後，狄倫和娜塔莉在市區的人行道上邊走邊聊天。

Dylan: Did I tell you that we were invited to a party at my office next month? It'll be formal, so we'll have to **dress up**[1].

Natalie: How exciting! I guess I'd better **look for**[2] some new clothes. Hey, let's go now to my favorite shop—it's not far from here. We can **look at**[3] that dress I told you about yesterday. However, I think it's pretty expensive.

Dylan: **Never mind**[4] the price. We can pay for it in installments, **little by little**[5]. It's important that we look great and impress my boss.

Natalie: Maybe I can **find out**[6] when they're having a sale. Then we could save some money.

Dylan: That's a good idea. After we check out that shop, let's go home. We've been walking around a lot, and, **as usual**[7], all this shopping has really **tired** me **out**[8].

狄倫： 我有提過我們受邀參加公司下個月的派對嗎？派對很正式，我們必須**盛裝打扮**。

娜塔莉： 真令人興奮！我想我最好**找**些新衣服。嘿，我們現在就去我最喜歡的那家店，就離這裡不遠。我們可以去**看**我昨天跟你提過的那件洋裝。不過我覺得它很貴。

狄倫： **別管**價格，我們可以**慢慢**用分期付款的。重要的是我們要看起來很體面，讓老闆印象深刻。

娜塔莉： 也許我能夠**查一下**何時會有折扣，這樣我們就可以省點錢了。

狄倫： 好主意。我們看完那家店就回家吧。我們已經走了好久，**就像往常一樣**，逛街真把我**累壞了**。

dress up 盛裝打扮

look for 尋找

9

1 **dress up** 特殊打扮；為正式場合盛裝打扮

- He **dressed up** as a cowboy for the party.
  他打扮成牛仔來參加派對。

- If you go to a wedding, it is important to **dress up**.
  盛裝參加婚禮很重要。

- Because Lucas didn't **dress up** for his job interview, he looked unprofessional.
  盧卡斯參加工作面試時沒有穿著正式服裝，所以看起來很不專業。

2 **look for** 尋找

- Pablo spent the entire morning **looking for** his car keys.
  帕布羅花了整個早上的時間尋找車鑰匙。

- The children walked all over the neighborhood **looking for** their lost dog.
  孩子們走遍整個街坊尋找走丟的小狗。

- He spent his life **looking for** the truth.
  他窮極一生都在追尋真理。

3 **look at** 注視；看

- Before his big date, Carl **looked at** himself carefully in the mirror.
  在赴重要約會前，卡爾仔細地注視著鏡中的自己。

look at 看著

4 never mind 別在意；不要緊

- **Never mind** your coming late; no one even noticed you weren't here.
  遲到沒關係，反正沒人注意到你不在這裡。

- My suggestion that you stay awake all night was a bad idea, so **never mind**.
  我提議整晚不睡是個爛主意，所以你別放在心上。

5 little by little 逐漸地

- **Little by little**, the kitten came to love and trust her new owner.
  小貓漸漸開始喜歡和依賴新主人了。

- At first I didn't like my math class, but **little by little**, I began to really enjoy it.
  我剛開始不喜歡數學課，但我逐漸得到其中真正的樂趣。

6 find out 發現；找出

- Last Monday, Jake **found out** that he was getting a promotion.
  傑克上星期一發現他升官了。

- I hope no one **finds out** about my embarrassing mistake!
  我希望沒人發現這個令人難堪的錯誤！

7 as usual 一如往常；照常

- Harry came to the meeting late, **as usual**.
  哈利照例開會遲到。

- **As usual**, Mom had prepared a delicious dinner for the family.
  我媽媽就像平常一樣為全家人準備美味的晚餐。

8 tire out 使筋疲力竭

- Gabe really **tired** himself **out** by walking around New York City all day.
  在紐約走了一天，蓋比筋疲力竭。

- We **tired out** the dogs by playing with them in the park for a few hours.
  我們和狗狗在公園裡玩了好幾個小時，把狗狗給累壞了。

9 call on 課堂上點名回答問題；請求；號召；呼籲；拜訪

- I was hoping Ms. Baker wouldn't **call on** me during history class because I didn't know the answer.
  希望貝克女士不要在歷史課指名我回答問題，因為我不知道答案。

- I now **call on** everyone to raise a glass to the happy couple.
  我現在請每一個人都舉起杯子，向這對幸福的新人致意。

- The university official **called on** the professors to help raise the school's reputation.
  學校高層號召教授幫忙提升學校的聲望。

- Scientists **have called on / will call on** the government to end political interference in science.
  科學家呼籲政府應該不要再對科學界做政治上的干涉。

- I will **call on** a friend this weekend.
  我這個週末會去拜訪一位朋友。

10 all right 沒問題；好吧；好的

- This book is **all right**, but it isn't anything special.
  這本書不錯，只是沒什麼特別之處。

- **All right**, so I made a mistake.
  好吧，是我的錯。

- Tell me if you start to feel sick, **all right**?
  如果你開始覺得不舒服，就跟我說好嗎？

- **All right**! They scored!
  好耶！得分！

- "**All right**, Mike?" "Not bad, thanks, and you?"
  「麥克你好嗎？」「還不錯，謝了。妳呢？」

11 all along 從一開始就；自始至終；一直

- We were shocked that Gloria had known about the late phone bill **all along** but hadn't told anyone.
  葛洛莉亞從一開始就知道電話帳單過期了，卻沒告訴任何人，令我們非常震驚。

- It was supposed to be a surprise party for Rudy, but actually he knew about it **all along**.
  這原本是要給魯迪的驚喜派對，但他事實上打從一開始就知道了。

- Do you think he's been cheating us **all along**?
  你想他是不是從一開始就在騙我們了？

Ron and Donna chat about a party this weekend.
朗和唐娜在聊有關這週末的派對。

Ron: Hey there, Donna! How are you doing?

Donna: Well, not so well. Actually, I **talked over**[1] my plan to go to your party this weekend with my parents, and they don't like the idea.

Ron: Really? I'm in no rush, so **take your time**[2] and tell me what the problem is.

Donna: Well, they are concerned that the party will be unsupervised. They also don't want me to stay out **all night long**[3].

Ron: But we won't be there **by ourselves**[4]; my parents will be there. Maybe if my dad called your mom to tell her this, it would **make a difference**[5] to her.

Donna: Yeah, maybe you're right. After all, our parents **get along with**[6] each other.

Ron: Exactly! Plus, the party won't go so late. You can be home before 11.

Donna: That will make my mom feel better.

Ron: Great! So why are you still **sitting down**[7]? **Stand up**[8], go home, and tell your mom that my dad will call later.

Donna: Okay, cool. See you soon!

朗： 嗨，唐娜！妳好嗎？

唐娜： 嗯，不怎麼好。事實上，我和我的父母**討論**過去參加你的週末派對的計畫，但他們不喜歡這個主意。

朗： 真的嗎？我不趕時間，所以**慢慢來**，告訴我問題在哪裡。

唐娜： 噯，他們認為派對裡沒大人看著，而且他們也不希望我**徹夜**未歸。

朗： 但又不是只有我們**獨**處而已，我的父母也會在。假如我爸打電話給妳媽，告訴她這點，對她或許**有所差別**。

唐娜： 是啊，也許你說的對。畢竟我們的父母很**處得來**。

朗： 沒錯！還有，派對不會到那麼晚，妳可以在 11 點前回到家。

唐娜： 我媽會覺得那樣比較好。

朗： 太好了！所以妳為何還**坐**在這裡？快**站起來**，回家告訴妳媽，我爸晚點會打電話過去。

唐娜： 對，好極了。改天見！

1   **talk over**   商量；討論

- There's no need to make a decision now; we can **talk it over** tomorrow.
  不用現在就做決定，我們可以明天再討論。
- Kerry **talked over** her request for a raise with her boss.
  凱莉和老闆商量要求加薪。

2   **take one's time**   慢慢來；別急

- **Take your time**; I'm in no rush.
  別急，我不趕時間。
- Bob didn't care that he was late; he continued to **take his time** eating his lunch.
  鮑伯不在乎遲到，他繼續慢慢吃午餐。

3   **all night long**   一整晚

- Lou stayed up **all night long** studying.
  盧整個晚上都在熬夜唸書。

4   **by oneself**   獨自；某人自己；單獨地

- Jenny's younger sister doesn't like to be left **by herself** for very long.
  珍妮的妹妹不喜歡長時間一個人獨處。

- The first day we left the puppy at home **by himself**, he made a big mess.
  我們第一次把小狗獨自留在家裡時，他把房子搞得一團糟。

5 make a difference 造成差別；對……產生影響

- Jill saw that cleaning her dorm **made a big difference** in how it looked.
  潔兒發現大掃除讓宿舍看起來截然不同。

- A healthy diet **makes a difference** in the way you feel. 健康的飲食會對身體產生影響。

- Sleeping an extra ten minutes a night **makes no difference** in how I feel the next morning.
  每晚多睡 10 分鐘，對我隔天早上的感覺不會有太大的影響。

6 get along (with) 和睦相處；進展

- Although Harry is a nice guy, for some reason Beth never **got along with** him.
  雖然哈利是個好人，但是基於某些原因，貝絲就是和他處不來。

- I wonder how Alex is **getting along** in his new job.
  不知亞力克斯的新工作做得如何。

7 sit down 坐下

- As soon as the teacher entered the classroom, all the students **sat down** and stopped talking.
  老師一走進教室，
  所有學生都坐下來停止說話。

8 stand up
站起來；經得住；
站得住腳；爽約

- After spending the entire day sitting in class, Paula said it felt good to **stand up** and walk around.
  寶拉覺得上課坐了一整天後，站起來走一走的感覺很舒服。

- Their evidence will never **stand up** in court.
  他們的證據在法庭上根本站不住腳。

- Xavier and I had a date for dinner, but he **stood** me **up**.
  傑維爾和我約好了要一起吃晚餐，結果他放我鴿子。

stand up 站起來

9 lie down 躺下

lie down 躺下

- Garth **lay down** on his bed and tried to sleep, but he couldn't.
  加爾斯躺在床上試圖入睡，但他睡不著。

- As soon as I **lay down**, I fell asleep.
  我一躺下來就睡著了。

10 pick out 挑選；辨認出

- When Terry arrived at the store, his father told him he could **pick out** any shirt he wanted.
  泰瑞到店裡時，父親要他挑選任何他想要的襯衫。

- Kim searched the audience for her friends but had trouble **picking** them **out** of the crowd.
  金在觀眾群中找尋朋友的蹤影，卻無法在人群中找到他們。

11 on purpose 刻意；有目的地

- I came late **on purpose**; it wasn't a mistake.
  我故意遲到，並不是誤會。

- Franz lost the card game **on purpose** because he wanted to go home.
  法蘭斯玩牌時故意輸掉，因為他想回家了。

12 take out 拿出來；和某人約會

- Mom asked me to **take out** the trash before I left.
  媽媽要我出門前把垃圾拿出去。

- The dentist **took** Jack's tooth **out**.
  牙醫拔掉傑克的牙齒。

- Warren **took** Lidia **out** for the first time last Friday.
  華倫和莉蒂亞上星期五第一次約會。

take out a tooth 拔牙

take out the trash 把垃圾拿出去

04

The School Play

學校戲劇表演

Mark and Cheryl have a conversation about the school play.

馬克和雪若正在談論學校的戲劇表演。

Mark: Did you hear about this year's school play?

Cheryl: No, tell me about it.

Mark: Well, it **takes place**[1] in London. If you're interested in learning more about it, you can **look** it **up**[2] online.

Cheryl: OK, it sounds cool. Are you **taking part in**[3] it?

Mark: Of course! In one scene, I work in a restaurant and **wait on**[4] the play's hero.

Cheryl: Wow! I'd like to be in the play, too—but I'm not a good actress **at all**[5].

Mark: Well, we are looking for **at least**[6] three more actors, so you should really consider it.

Cheryl: All right. I'll **think** it **over**[7].

Mark: OK, but don't think too much! Anyway, I'd better go and **try on**[8] my costume.

Cheryl: See you, and good luck!

馬克： 妳聽説今年學校的戲劇表演了嗎？

雪若： 沒有，説來聽聽。

馬克： 嗯，它會在倫敦**舉行**。如果妳有興趣想知道更多訊息，可以上網**查詢**。

雪若： 好，聽起來不錯。你會**參加**嗎？

馬克： 當然！我在一個餐廳的場景中，負責**接待**劇中的男主角。

雪若： 哇！我也想參與演出，但是我的演技**一點也**不好。

馬克： 喔，我們還在找**最少**三位演員，妳真的應該考慮看看。

雪若： 嗯，我會**仔細考慮**的。

馬克： 好，但別想太多！總之，我最好去**試穿**我的戲服了。

雪若： 再見，祝你好運！

look up 查詢　　　　　　　wait on 接待

21

1   **take place** 舉行；發生

- The party will **take place** in two weeks.
  派對會在兩個星期後舉行。

- When does the class **take place**?
  那堂課何時開始？

- Not all engineering failures **take place** suddenly and dramatically.
  工程問題的發生，不一定都是很突然很劇烈的。

2   **look up** 查詢（字典等）；仰視；轉好；拜訪

- If you don't know what a word means, just **look** it **up** in the dictionary.
  如果不知道某個生字的意思，就查字典。

- She **looked up** from her book as I entered the room.
  我進屋時，她停下看書抬眼看了一下。

- I hope things start to **look up** in the new year.
  希望新的一年情況會開始好轉。

- **Look** me **up** next time you're in Paris.
  下次來巴黎時要來找我喔。

3   **take part in** 參加；參與

- Will you **take part in** the school musical this year?
  你會參加學校今年的歌舞劇嗎？

- The teacher told us that it would help our grades if we **took part in** class discussions.
  老師說我們如果參與課堂討論，對分數會很有幫助。

take part in 參與

4　**wait on**　（服務生或店員的）服務；接待

- Although the food wasn't very good, the young woman who **waited on** us at the restaurant was very nice.
  雖然這家餐廳的食物不是很好吃，但是接待我們的女服務生很親切。

wait on 服務

- We sat for twenty minutes before we were **waited on**.
  我們坐了 20 分鐘才有服務生來點餐。

5　**at all**　絲毫；根本

- There's nothing left in the house **at all**; everything has been moved out.
  房子裡什麼也沒有，所有東西都被搬光了。

- The police asked Marty why he ran away from them, but he had nothing **at all** to say.
  警察詢問馬堤為何逃跑，但他絲毫無話可說。

6　**at least**　至少

- When you are at the store, please pick up **at least** three pounds of onions.
  請你到商店買至少三磅的洋蔥。

- When I have a family, I want **at least** two children.
  等有了家庭後，我最少想要兩個小孩。

7 think over 仔細考慮；深思熟慮

- Jan wasn't sure if it was a good idea to buy the car, so she **thought** it **over** for a few days.
  珍不確定買車是否是個好主意，所以她仔細考慮了好幾天。

- After **thinking over** the assignment, Marion got started with her research.
  瑪莉安在認真思索過這份工作後便開始進行研究。

think over 仔細考慮

8 try on 試穿

try on 試穿

- Before you buy those jeans, **try** them **on** to make sure they fit.
  買牛仔褲前，記得要試穿以便確定是否合身。

- If you don't have any nice shoes to wear with your suit, you can **try on** mine; if they fit, you can borrow them.
  你若是沒有好看的鞋能搭套裝，可以試穿我的，如果合腳，你可以借去穿。

9 take a walk (stroll, hike, etc.) 散步；閒逛

- After a large dinner, Tracy likes to **take a stroll** around the park.
  崔西喜歡在用過豐盛的晚餐後到公園裡散步。

- Last weekend, Franz and his family went on a picnic and then **took a hike** in the nearby hills.
  法蘭斯上星期和家人去野餐，然後在附近的山區健行。

take a walk 散步

10　take a trip 遠行；旅行

- Reg won't come in to work next week because he's **taking a trip** to Chicago for a business meeting.
雷格下星期不會來上班，因為他要到芝加哥出差開會。

take a trip 旅行

- This summer, Barbra plans to **take a trip** to Mexico.
芭芭拉計畫這個夏天到墨西哥旅行。

11　put away 收拾；收起來；儲存；大吃特吃

- James told his little sister to **put away** all her toys before their parents got home.
詹姆斯叫妹妹在父母回來前把玩具收拾好。

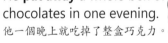

- The teacher told me to **put** my cell phone **away** because I was using it during class.
我上課時在用手機，老師要我把它收起來。

- I decided to **put away** a few dollars each week.
我決定每個星期都要存下一點錢。

- He **put away** a whole box of chocolates in one evening.
他一個晚上就吃掉了整盒巧克力。

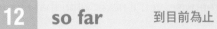

12　so far 到目前為止

- My first semester at college is going well **so far**—though we haven't had any tests yet.
我在大學的第一個學期到目前為止都很順利，儘管我們還沒考過試。

- **So far** during this car ride, we've passed three gas stations without stopping.
到目前為止，我們已經開車經過了三間加油站，但都沒有停下來。

25

Joe and Erin talk about schoolwork.
喬和愛琳在談論學校功課。

Joe: Have you finished writing your history paper yet?

Erin: No, I've been **putting** it **off**[1] until I **get over**[2] this illness.

Joe: What's wrong? Did you **catch a cold**[3]?

Erin: Yeah. I spent a weekend taking care of my sick aunt, by the time I **got back**[4] I was already feeling bad.

Joe: Well, I hope you get better soon.

Erin: Thanks. I'm taking it easy **for the time being**[5]; however, I am thinking about going to the movies tonight with my boyfriend.

Joe: I see. You know, I think you should **change your mind**[6]—otherwise, you'll never write that history paper!

Erin: You may be right, but it's too late. I've already **made up my mind**[7] to go out. There's no way I'm going to **call off**[8] my date!

Joe: Well, what can I say? Good luck!

喬： 妳的歷史報告寫完了嗎？

愛琳： 還沒，我一直**拖**到**病好了**才開始趕作業。

喬： 怎麼回事？妳**感冒**了嗎？

愛琳： 沒錯，我上週末照顧生病的阿姨，在**回家路上**就已經覺得不舒服了。

喬： 嗯，希望妳早日康復。

愛琳： 謝謝，我**現在**感覺還可以，不過我今晚想和男朋友去看場電影。

喬： 我知道了。我跟妳說，我覺得妳最好**改變主意**，否則妳永遠別想寫歷史報告了！

愛琳： 也許你是對的，不過太遲了，我已經**決定**要出去了，絕對不可能**取消**約會！

喬： 嗯，那我能說什麼呢？祝妳好運！

catch a cold 感冒

make up one's mind 決定

27

1   put off   拖延；延期

- Never **put off** till tomorrow what you can do today.
  今日事今日畢。〔俗諺〕

- If you **put off** writing this essay until the weekend, I'm sure you'll regret it.
  如果你拖到週末才寫報告，你一定會後悔的。

- Rudy didn't want to go to the doctor; however, when he woke up with a terrible headache, he realized he couldn't **put it off** any longer.
  魯迪不想去看醫生，但當他頭疼欲裂地醒來時，他知道看醫生一事無法再拖下去了。

2   get over   （從生病、悲傷中）復原；恢復

- It took Martin a few days to **get over** failing the final exam.
  馬汀花了好幾天才走出期末考不及格的陰影。

- The day Wendy **got over** the infection, she returned to work.
  溫蒂在病情好轉的那天回到工作崗位。

- It took him months to **get over** Nicole after she ended the relationship.
  在妮可提出分手之後，他花了好幾個月的時間才把她給忘了。

3   catch (a) cold   感冒（喉嚨痛、輕微咳嗽、流鼻涕）

- Miranda missed class because she **caught a cold**.
  米蘭達因感冒而未去上課。

- Every winter, Vince **catches** at least one **cold**.
  文斯每年冬天至少會感冒一次。

4 get back 取回；回來

- Mandy **gets back** from work around 3 o'clock or so.
  曼蒂約三點下班回到家。

- Can you please **get** my MP3 player **back** from Janet?
  你可以幫我向珍娜拿回我的 MP3 嗎？

5 for the time being 現在；目前

- **For the time being**, the students don't have any questions, but they may feel differently tomorrow.
  學生現在沒有任何問題，但明天可能就不一樣了。

- I'm not hungry **for the time being**, but by noon I'll be starving.
  我現在不餓，不過中午前就會餓了。

6 change one's mind 改變主意

- My girlfriend always **changes her mind** a few times before making a big decision.
  在下重大決定前，我的女朋友總會三番兩次地改變心意。

- You'd better be sure this is the car you want because once you agree to buy it, you can't **change your mind**.
  你最好確定這台車就是你想要的，因為一旦你同意買下它，就無法改變主意了。

- When I first met him, I didn't like him; however, since then I've **changed my mind**.
  第一次和他見面的時候，我並不喜歡他，但後來我的看法改變了。

7   make up one's mind   下定決心；決定

- There are so many flavors of ice cream here that it is hard to **make up my mind** and choose one.
  這裡有好多種口味的冰淇淋，我很難決定要選哪一種。

- Ralph couldn't **make up his mind** about going to the park or not.
  瑞夫無法決定是否要去公園。

- Gwen can't **make up her mind** about whether to visit L.A. or Miami this summer.
  關無法決定今年夏天要去洛杉磯還是邁阿密。

8   call off   取消（會議、事件）；叫走

- Because it was raining, Diane **called off** the outdoor volleyball competition.
  下雨了，黛安取消了戶外排球比賽。

- The CEO **called off** the meeting and told his employees to go home early.
  執行長取消了會議，要員工早點回家。

- Tomorrow's match has been **called off** because of the weather.
  由於天氣寒冷的緣故，明天的比賽已經取消了。

call off 取消

30

9　look out　小心；注意

- **Look out!** The teacher is coming, and he'll see that you are skipping class.
  小心點！老師快要來了，
  他會發現你翹課。

- If you travel alone at night, be sure to **look out** for robbers.
  晚上單獨出門，要留意搶匪。

look out for robbers 留意搶匪

10　shake hands　握手

- In America, it is important to **shake hands** firmly or people will think you have a weak personality.
  在美國，握手時把手握緊很重要，
  否則別人會認為你的個性軟弱。

11　for good　永遠地；永久地

- After the graduation ceremony, Lou knew that he was done with high school **for good**.
  畢業典禮過後，盧知道他的高中生活永遠結束了。

Getting Sick and Stressed
生病與壓力

Didi tells her friend Jay why she is feeling sick and a
bit stressed. 蒂蒂把感覺不舒服和緊張的原因告訴朋友傑。

Jay: What's wrong? You look a bit **under the weather**[1].

Didi: As a matter of fact, I'm not feeling so good. I just started classes in a new school, and it isn't easy **making friends**[2].

Jay: Don't worry about that! It takes time to meet people. You need to focus on feeling better.

Didi: Well, the other thing that is stressing me out is that someone keeps calling my cell, and when I answer, the person **hangs up**[3] without saying a word. I just don't know what's **going on**[4].

Jay: Oh, man! I'm sure that really **gets to**[5] you; but you know what I think? I bet somebody has a crush on you and is too scared to talk.

Didi: Really? I never thought about that before. **All of a sudden**[6], I feel a bit better. I can always **count on**[7] you to make me feel more positive.

Jay: No problem. Good people like you are **few and far between**[8]. You deserve to be happy and calm.

under the weather 生病

傑： 怎麼了？妳看起來有點像是**生病**了。

蒂蒂： 事實上，我覺得不太舒服。我剛到新學校上課，**交朋友**不太容易。

傑： 別擔心！那是需要時間的。妳需要集中注意力在保持好心情。

蒂蒂： 嗯，還有一件讓我很緊張的事情，就是有人一直打我的手機。當我接起來時，對方不說話就**把電話掛掉**，我不知道**發生**了什麼事情。

傑： 噢，我敢肯定妳一定很**困擾**，妳知道我的看法嗎？我打賭一定是有人愛上妳了，而且還不敢開口。

蒂蒂： 真的嗎？我從來沒想過這些。我**突然**覺得好多了，都是**靠**你幫忙，我才能往好的方面去想。

傑： 沒什麼，像妳這麼好的人已經**很少**了，妳本來就應該要快樂平靜。

make friends 交朋友

hang up 掛斷（電話）

1 **under the weather** 身體不舒服；生病

- Walt canceled the discussion group because he was feeling a bit **under the weather**.
  華特因為身體不舒服，取消了團體討論。

- After a long day of walking in the cold rain, Roberta felt a little **under the weather**.
  羅伯特在寒冷的雨中走了一天，感覺身體有點不舒服。

2 **make friends** 交朋友

- Because Pam was new at the school, it took her a couple of weeks to **make friends**.
  潘是新生，所以她花了好幾個星期才交到朋友。

- Mark is a great guy, so he **makes** new **friends** easily.
  馬克是一個很棒的人，所以很容易交到新朋友。

- I've **made** a lot of **friends** at this job.
  這份工作讓我結交到許多朋友。

3 **hang up** 懸掛（衣服）；掛斷電話

- Ray **hung up** all his clean shirts in the closet.
  雷把所有乾淨的襯衫掛在衣櫥裡。

- Joel was so mad at his cousin that he **hung up** without saying goodbye.
  喬爾很氣他的表弟沒說再見就掛掉電話。

hang up 掛斷電話

4

4

4 **go on** 發生；繼續下去

- Do you know what's **going on** with your son in L.A.?
  你知道你的兒子在洛杉磯發生了什麼事情嗎？

- By the time Frank arrived at the meeting, it had already been **going on** for a few minutes.
  法蘭克到達時，會議已經進行了好幾分鐘。

5 **get to** 可以做（某事）；到達；感到困擾

- If Beth gets an "A" on her history test, her mom said she'll **get to** have a party.
  如果貝絲歷史考試得到「A」，媽媽說她就可以舉辦派對。

- The barking dog was really **getting to** me, so I called my neighbor and asked her to do something about it.
  我覺得那隻狂吠的狗很煩，所以我打電話給鄰居要她處理一下。

- When do you think we'll **get to** the city center?
  你覺得我們什麼時候會到達市中心？

6 **all of a sudden** 突然；毫無預警

- **All of a sudden**, it started raining and we got wet.
  天空突然開始下起雨，我們淋濕了。

- Lucy was shocked when Evan asked her **all of a sudden** to marry him.
  艾文突然向露西求婚，令她非常震驚。

7   count on   依靠；指望；相信

- If you ever need help, remember that you can **count on** me.
  如果你需要幫忙，記住你可以相信我。

- Ryan knows that he can **count on** his uncle to meet him at the airport.
  雷恩相信叔叔會在機場和他見面。

8   few and far between   稀有；獨特

- Good Indian restaurants are **few and far between** in Austin .
  奧斯汀好吃的印度餐廳很少。

- These days, stores that sell tape players are **few and far between** because everyone prefers CDs and MP3 players.
  現在販售錄音機的店已經很少了，因為大家偏好 CD 和 MP3。

- Apartments that are both comfortable and reasonably priced are **few and far between**.
  既舒適、價錢又合理的公寓並不多。

9   look over   檢查；查看

- Before buying a used car, **look** it **over** very carefully to be sure it doesn't have any problems.
  買二手車前，記得要仔細檢查，才能確定車子沒有任何問題。

- Ms. Perry **looked over** the students' papers before grading them.
  派瑞女士在打分數前，仔細檢查學生的報告。

10 out of order （機器）故障；行為失常

- The snack machine at the office was **out of order**, so we went to a restaurant for lunch.
  辦公室裡的點心販賣機故障了，所以我們到餐廳吃午餐。

- The sign on the pay phone informed Tina that it was **out of order**.
  緹娜由公共電話上的標示得知電話故障了。

out of order 故障

- The remark Harry made in the workshop yesterday was totally **out of order**.
  哈利昨天在研討會所做的評論完全錯誤。

11 put out 拿出去；關閉；熄滅；打擾；推出

- Dad asked me to **put out** the trash.
  爸爸要我把垃圾拿出去。

- Please **put** the lights **out** before you leave the house. 出門前請把燈關掉。

- The campers poured water on the fire to **put** it **out**.
  露營的人用水把火澆熄。

put out a fire 滅火

12 take (time) off （一段時間）不工作；休假

- My wife's birthday is next Monday, so if possible, I'd like to **take** that day **off** of work.
  下星期一是我老婆的生日，可以的話，那天我想要休假。

- The companies let the workers **take off** two weeks every year for vacation and holidays.
  這家公司的員工每年都有兩個星期的假期。

Hunting for a New Job
找新工作 🎧 019

Steve tells Caroline why he wants a new job.
史帝夫告訴卡洛琳想要新工作的原因。

Caroline: You've been quiet all weekend. I can't **figure out**[1] what's bothering you.

Steve: I'm just thinking about my job. I don't like it so much. For one thing, I need to **be up**[2] at 5 a.m. if I want to get to the office **on time**[3]. And work **isn't over**[4] until 7 p.m.

Caroline: Oh! That sounds tough. What happens if you **get sick**[5]?

Steve: My boss always makes me come in, no matter how sick I am.

Caroline: Now I see why you're **thinking of**[6] looking for another job.

Steve: Sometimes I **would rather**[7] not work at all, but then my sister **points out**[8] that I shouldn't leave this job before I find another one.

Caroline: I think she's right.

卡洛琳：	你整個週末都好安靜。我**想**不透你在煩惱什麼？
史帝夫：	我只是在想我的工作。我不是很喜歡我的工作。首先，我若想要**準時**上班，必須早上五點**起床**，然後一直工作到晚上七點才**結束**。
卡洛琳：	噢！聽起來真難熬。**生病**的話怎麼辦？
史帝夫：	無論我的病情有多嚴重，老闆總是要我去上班。
卡洛琳：	我知道你為何**想**找別的工作了。
史帝夫：	我有時候**寧願**完全不工作，但我姐姐**指出**，在我找到其他工作前，不應該辭掉這份工作。
卡洛琳：	我想她說的對。

get sick 生病　　on time 準時

1 figure out 找出答案；解決問題

- No one could **figure out** how Darryl lost his keys.
  沒人知道戴倫是如何弄丟鑰匙的。

- Every student looked at the puzzles, but no one could **figure** them **out**.
  每位學生都看著文字填空的題目，但沒人找得出答案。

- Laura couldn't **figure out** how she spent all her money.
  蘿拉想不透她是如何花光所有的錢。

2 be up 醒來；（時間）到了

- Janet can't stay out too late tonight because she has to **be up** at 5 in the morning.
  珍娜今晚不能在外面待到太晚，因為她必須早上五點起床。

- Although Gwen pretended to be asleep, she **was** really **up**.
  雖然關假裝睡著了，但她其實是醒著的。

- The teacher told us when the time for the test **was up** and we had to put our pencils down.
  老師說考試結束時，我們必須把鉛筆放下。

3 on time 準時；依照時間

- Marianne never arrives anywhere **on time**; she's always late.
  瑪莉安從來沒有準時過，她老是遲到。

- This bus is always **on time**, so you can rely on it.
  這班公車總是很準時，非常靠得住。

```
12:55 AM S9    On-Time
9:35 PM C10    On-Time
5:15 AM A13    On-Time
9:30 PM D5     On-Time
11:30 PM S4    On-Time
9:09 PM A13    On-Time
5:30 PM B14    Now 6:15 PM
6:15 PM B10    On-Time
```

on time 準時

4   be over   結束

- What time **is** this show **over**? 這場表演何時會結束？
- French class **is over** before lunch. 法文課會在午餐前結束。

5   get sick   生病

- The old man **got sick** while he was away and had to come home.
  那位老先生在外面的時候生病了，所以必須回家。

6   think of   想到；對某人產生評價

- Suddenly, Jon **thought of** a great idea for his new book and got to work.
  強突然想到一個關於新書很棒的主意，並且開始進行。
- What do you **think of** the new mayor?
  你覺得新上任的市長如何？
- Meredith was new in our class, so no one knew what to **think of** her.
  瑪芮迪絲是我們班上的新生，所以沒有人對她作出評論。

7   would rather   寧願

- Instead of going shopping today, I'**d** much **rather** stay home and watch TV.
  與其要我今天去逛街，我寧願待在家裡看電視。
- **Would** you **rather** live in Florida or Georgia?
  你比較想住在佛羅里達州還是喬治亞州？

8   point out   指出;提醒

- Tory **pointed out** her sister to us.
  托莉把她的姐姐指給我們看。

- Before his mom **pointed out** that today is Friday, Wayne thought he had to go to school tomorrow.
  在偉恩的媽媽指出今天是星期五前,他一直以為隔天還要上課。

point out 指出

- I thought that my English was perfect, but my teacher **pointed** my mistakes **out**.
  我以為我的英文很通順,但老師指出了我的錯誤。

9   in time   及時……

- If we don't leave now, you won't get to the airport **in time** to catch your flight.
  我們若不現在離開,你就無法及時趕到機場登機。

- Sean needs to be home **in time** to meet his sister.
  西恩必須及時趕回家,才能和他的姐姐碰面。

10 **call it a day** 結束當天的工作；到此為止

- After spending the entire morning and afternoon working on her report, Liana decided to **call it a day**.
  黎安娜整個早上和下午都在忙報告，她決定今天就到此為止。

11 **get better** 使情況好轉

- Despite practicing every day, George never really **got better** at the piano.
  儘管喬治每天練習，
  但他的鋼琴技巧卻不見進步。

She is **getting better** now.
她身體逐漸好轉。

12 **had better** 應該；最好

- If you want to go to Yale, you'**d better** study more.
  如果你想進入耶魯，最好多讀點書。

- Sam **had better** practice the flute every day if he wants to play in an orchestra.
  如果山姆想要進入管絃樂隊，最好每天練習吹長笛。

Planning for the Weekend 週末計畫

Douglas and Mary consider how to spend their weekend.
道格拉斯和瑪麗在考慮如何度過這個週末。

Mary: Let's go to the opera this weekend! It's from Italy, and it'll be a good chance for me to **brush up on**[1] my Italian.

Douglas: I know we said that we would **take turns**[2] deciding what to do on the weekends, and even though it's your turn, I was hoping we could **go out**[3] and see a baseball game.

Mary: Well, you need to **pay attention to**[4] the weather; it's supposed to rain, so going to see the game is totally **out of the question**[5].

Douglas: Who cares about a little rain?

Mary: I've told you **over and over again**[6] that I hate getting cold and wet.

Douglas: Well, I **was about to**[7] buy the tickets online— but if you're sure you don't want to go, I guess the opera won't be so bad. However, I don't think there are hot dogs at the opera.

opera 歌劇

瑪麗：	我們這週末去看歌劇吧！那是一齣義大利歌劇，對我來說，這會是一個**複習**義大利文的好機會。
道格拉斯：	我知道我們説好要**輪流**決定週末要做些什麼，不過就算這星期是輪到你決定，我還是希望我們可以**出去**看籃球比賽。
瑪麗：	噢，你必須多**注意**天氣。那天可能會下雨，所以絕對**不可能**去看比賽的。
道格拉斯：	下毛毛雨有什麼關係？
瑪麗：	我**一再**告訴你，我討厭變冷和被淋濕。
道格拉斯：	嗳，我**正要**上網買票。但妳如果真的不想去，我想歌劇也不是個太差的主意。不過，我認為歌劇院裡不會有賣熱狗。

opera house 歌劇院

go out 外出

45

1 brush up on 複習

- I really need to **brush up on** my Japanese before visiting Tokyo next month.
  我真的需要在下個月去東京前，複習一下我的日文。

- Ivan **brushed up on** Greek history before the test.
  艾文在考試前複習希臘歷史。

- **Brushing up on** computer skills is important for anyone who is thinking about getting a new job.
  複習電腦技能對想換新工作的人來說很重要。

2 take turns 輪流

- When the kids play on the swings, we try to make sure they **take turns**.
  他們在盪鞦韆的時候，我們試著讓每個孩子輪流玩。

- Ariel and Mac **took turns** using the laptop.
  艾芮兒和麥可輪流使用筆記型電腦。

3 go out 離開（家、學校、辦公室）外出；熄滅

- We usually **go out** on the weekends and have dinner or see a movie.
  我們週末通常都會出去吃晚餐或看電影。

- Do you want to **go out** after work today?
  你今天下班後想要出去嗎？

- When the fire **went out**, it started to get cold.
  火熄滅後就開始變冷了。

4 pay attention (to) 注意；專心

- It's no wonder you didn't pass the test; you never **pay attention to** what the professor is saying.
  難怪你沒通過考試，你從不注意教授說的話。

- Don't **pay** any **attention to** what that woman says; she's crazy.
  別去注意那女人說的話，她瘋了。

5 out of the question 不可能發生

- Unless I pay for the trip myself, going to Boston is **out of the question**.
  除非我自己出錢，否則波士頓之旅是不可能成行的。

- Buying that huge TV is totally **out of the question** unless I win the lottery.
  除非我中樂透，否則絕對不可能買那台大電視。

6 over and over (again) 一再；再三

- I hate to do the same work **over and over**.
  我討厭反覆做同樣的工作。

- The little boy kept asking **over and over** if I'd buy him some candy.
  那個小男孩一再問我是否會買一些糖果給他。

- Ed read the article **over and over again** until he finally understood the main idea.
  艾德把文章讀了一遍又一遍，直到他終於了解重點。

- I read the article **over and over** till it made sense.
  我把文章看過一遍又一遍，直到看懂為止。

7   be about to   正要去做；準備去做

- I **was** just **about to** leave the house when the phone rang.
  當我正要出門時，電話響了。

- What **were** you **about to** do when the Martins arrived?
  馬汀一家來的時候你原本要做什麼？

8   have to do with   與……有關；在不同的情況（困境）中生存

- This conversation doesn't **have to do with** you, so please go away.
  這段談話與你無關，所以請你走開。

- The restaurant didn't have any cake, so Joe **had to do with** the fruit salad.
  這家餐廳沒有蛋糕，所以喬只好吃水果沙拉。

- When Esther lost her job, she **had to** learn to **do with** less.
  當愛絲特丟了工作，她必須學會在困境中生存。

9   wear out   穿舊；用壞；耗盡

- If you don't turn the digital camera off when you're not using it, you'll **wear out** the batteries quickly.
  不使用數位相機時若沒有關閉，電池很快會耗盡。

- I love these jeans so much, but it's only a matter of time before they **wear out**.
  我很喜歡這件牛仔褲，但它遲早會被穿壞。

wear out 穿舊

10 throw away 扔掉;浪費(才能或機會)

- Those old shirts really smell terrible; maybe you should just **throw** them **away**.
  那些舊襯衫的味道真的很難聞,
  也許你該把它們丟了。

- You've spent four hours studying—don't **throw** it all **away**.
  你已經唸了四小時了,千萬不要白白浪費了。

throw away 扔掉

11 turn around 轉向;使情勢徹底改觀

- When Ike **turned around**, he saw that the puppy was following him home.
  艾克轉身發現那隻小狗在跟他回家。

- As soon as Rachel realized that she had forgotten her camera, she **turned** the car **around** and went back home.
  芮秋一發現忘了帶相機,就將車掉頭回家。

- When the weather got better, the entire weekend **turned around,** and we finally had a good time at the beach.
  整個週末隨著天空放晴而改變,我們於是在海邊度過了一段愉快的時光。

12 fall in love 墜入情網

- Four weeks after **falling in love** with Maria, Jack asked her to marry him.
  傑克和瑪麗亞墜入愛河四星期後,
  他便向她求婚了。

fall in love 墜入情網

- As soon as Verona saw Sid, she **fell in love**. 薇諾娜一見到希德便愛上他了。

🎧025

Writing
a Children's Book 童書創作

Grace tells John about her ideas for an upcoming children's book. 葛芮絲把有關新童書的想法告訴約翰。

Grace: Good morning, John! Why are you so sleepy?

John: Well, when you **got in touch with**[1] me this morning to invite me out for coffee, you **woke** me **up**[2].

Grace: I'm sorry about that! Actually, I wanted to see you right away because I'd like you to help me write a children's book. I know you're a great artist, so I want you to **be in charge of**[3] the drawings in the book. Can you do that?

John: Sure. I'll have a lot of time **as soon as**[4] I finish classes next week. This sounds like a fun project. I bet I'll **have a good time**[5] working with you.

Grace: I think you will. Together, we'll have the entire book finished **in no time**[6]. Have you ever done anything like this before?

John: Well, I **used to**[7] draw cartoons for a comic book, so it shouldn't be hard to **get used to**[8] this kind of project.

Grace: Perfect!

get in touch with 聯絡

葛芮絲： 早安，約翰！為什麼你這麼沒精神？

約翰： 唔，妳今天早上和我**聯絡**、約我出去喝咖啡時，把我**吵醒**了。

葛芮絲： 真是抱歉！事實上，我當時急著找你，是因為我希望你能幫我寫一本童書。我知道你是一個很棒的畫家，所以想要請你**負責**書中的插畫。可以嗎？

約翰： 當然。只要**一**結束下星期的課，我**就**會有許多時間。這聽起來是一個很有趣的案子。我相信和你合作會**很愉快的**。

葛芮絲： 沒錯。我們**很快**就會一起完成整本書。你曾經做過類似的工作嗎？

約翰： 嗯，我**以前**畫過卡通漫畫，所以要**適應**這件案子並不難。

葛芮絲： 太棒了！

have a good time 很愉快

51

1 **get in touch with** 與……聯絡

- Verona will **get in touch with** you as soon as she hears some news.
薇諾娜一有消息就會和你聯絡。

- It's been years since he **got in touch with** my cousin.
他已經和我表哥聯絡了好幾年。

2 **wake up** 醒來；使警覺

- What time did you **wake up** this morning?
你今天早上幾點起床？

- Companies need to **wake up** and take notice of the public's increasing concerns about the environment.
公司必須有所警覺，注意民眾有越來越關心環境問題的趨勢。

wake up 醒來

3 **be in charge of** 負責；管理

- Emily **is in charge of** the class pet this week.
艾蜜莉這星期要負責照顧班上的寵物。

- Jeremy is the football team's coach, so he'**s in charge of** making sure the players perform well.
傑諾米是足球隊的教練，所以他負責確保球員都能有好的表現。

4   as soon as 立即；一……就……

- I'll call you **as soon as** I can.
  我會儘快打電話給你。

- **As soon as** I opened the door, I knew there was a problem.
  我一開門，就知道有問題。

5   have a good time 玩得愉快

- Did you **have a good time** at the concert last weekend?
  你在上週末的演唱會中玩得愉快嗎？

have a good time 玩得愉快

- My older sister **had a good time** at the park because the weather was perfect.
  天氣很好，我姐姐在公園玩得很愉快。

6   in no time 很快地；立刻

- The book was so interesting that the students finished it **in no time**.
  這本書非常有趣，學生很快就看完了。

- Dylan had been thinking about his Greek history report for several days, so when he started working, he finished it **in no time**.
  狄倫過去幾天一直在思索希臘歷史報告，所以他開始不久後，很快便完成了。

- I pulled my blanket around me, and **in no time**, I was fast asleep.
  我蓋上毯子後很快地便進入夢鄉。

7 used to 過去經常；過去習慣

- Betty **used to** teach English, but now she has a different job.
  貝蒂曾是英文老師，但她現在找到了一份不同的工作。

- I **used to** go for a jog every morning, but then it got too cold outside.
  我以前時常每天早上去散步，但後來天氣變冷了。

8 get used to 逐漸適應；習慣於

- At first, Natalie didn't like sushi; but after living in Tokyo for a few weeks, she **got used to** it.
  娜塔莉一開始不喜歡壽司，但她在東京住了幾個星期後便習慣了。

9 cut down on 削減；減少

- Because Dean was trying to lose weight, he **cut down on** the number of snacks he ate.
  狄恩想要減重，所以他減少吃零食。

- If you want to **cut down on** the amount of money you spend at the supermarket, never shop when you're hungry.
  如果想要在超市少花點錢，就別在肚子餓的時候去買東西。

10 back and forth 來來回回

- The wind made the boat rock **back and forth** on the water.
  風把船吹得搖搖晃晃。

- Because Rachel wanted to get in shape, she ran **back and forth** across the field every morning.
  瑞秋想要好身材，所以每天早上來來回回地在操場上跑步。

11 quite a few 許多;相當多
（介於 a few 和 a lot 之間）

- Casey wanted to make his own apple juice, applesauce, and apple pie, so he bought **quite a few** pounds of apples at the market.

  凱西想要自己做蘋果汁、蘋果醬和蘋果派，所以他到市場買了好幾磅的蘋果。

- There was a big sale at the bookstore, so Floyd bought **quite a few** books.

  書店在大減價，所以佛洛伊德買了許多書。

a few 不多

quite a few 許多

12 be used to 已經習慣於……;熟悉

- Joan **is used to** horses, so she wasn't scared of riding one.

  瓊已經習慣了馬兒，所以她不害怕騎馬。

- I **am used to** cooking my own dinner.

  我已經習慣自己準備晚餐了。

Choosing a Pet

挑選寵物 [028]

Ava and Ethan are choosing a pet in a pet store.
愛娃和伊森正在寵物店挑選寵物。

Ethan: OK, Ava. We have to **make sure**[1] that we get a pet we'll be happy with and won't ever want to **get rid of**[2].

Ava: That's true! A pet is not something we can take care of **now and then**[3]; it's a big commitment.

Ethan: How about that white rat? His white fur will **go with**[4] your white jacket.

Ava: No way! Oh, look at those kittens playing together. Look at that one there; he's really cute.

Ethan: I agree. Let's buy him! But before we take him home, we should **see about**[5] getting some cat food and some toys for him before the stores close.

Ava: Okay, but let's go now. If we **make good time**[6], we can get back to the pet store quickly. I don't want anyone else to take our kitten!

伊森： 好了，愛娃，記得**確定**要選一隻我們滿意的寵物，而且永遠不要**丟棄**它。

愛娃： 沒錯！養寵物並不是**偶爾**照顧一下而已，而是一項承諾。

伊森： 這隻白老鼠如何？他身上的白毛和你的白色夾克很**配**。

愛娃： 不要！噢，看那些玩在一起的小貓。你看那邊那隻，好可愛噢。

伊森： 我也這麼認為。我們就買他吧！但是帶他回家之前，我們應該**考慮**在商店打烊前去買一些貓食和玩具給他。

愛娃： 好，不過我們現在就走吧。我們如果**走快**一點，就能夠趕快回到寵物店。我不希望有人買走我們的小貓！

1   make sure 確定;確認

- Before you leave the house, **make sure** that you turn all the lights off.

  出門前，要確認所有的燈都關了。

- I need to **make sure** that I call my parents if I'm going to be late.

  若是要晚歸，我一定要確定先打電話給爸媽。

2   get rid of 去除;丟棄

- How do I **get rid of** all these ants in my house?

  我該如何消除屋內所有的螞蟻？

- Drinking herbal tea will help you **get rid of** your sore throat.

  飲用花草茶能幫助你消除喉嚨痛。

3   now and then 有時候;偶爾

- We meet up **now and then**, maybe once every few months.

  我們偶爾會見面，大概幾個月見一次面。

- Call your parents **now and then** and let them know you care.

  偶爾打電話給你的父母，讓他們知道你很關心他們。

- Every **now and then** I'll take the kids to the playground.

  我有時候會帶孩子們去遊樂場玩。

4 go with 與……搭配（通常指衣服、食物）；與……交往；與……看法相同

- That orange tie definitely does not **go with** that pink shirt!

  那條橘色領帶顯然和粉紅色襯衫不太相配！

- Do you think red or white wine **goes with** this lasagna?

  你覺得這道千層麵要配紅酒或白酒呢？

5 see about 留意；安排；關照；考慮

- I'm not sure if Carla is coming to the party; I'd better **see about** sending her an invitation.

  我不確定卡拉是否會來參加派對，我打算寄邀請卡給她。

- My dad said he was going to **see about** buying me a motorcycle.

  我老爸說他打算買一台摩托車給我。

6 make good time 很快地結束旅行；做事快速

- Although we left later than planned, we **made good time** and arrived before the show started.

  雖然我們比計畫中還要晚離開，但我們速度很快，所以到達時並不會太晚。

- We **made good time** driving to Taipei because the traffic was light.

  由於路況順暢，我們很快就開車到達台北。

7 by heart   記住（詩、歌、故事）

- Annabelle loves *Hamlet*; she knows most of the famous lines **by heart**.
  安娜貝爾最愛《哈姆雷特》，
  她記住了大部分有名的詩詞。

- Jack studied his lines in the play until he was sure he knew them **by heart**.
  傑克一直在背他在劇中的臺詞，
  直到他確定都記住了。

learn the words by heart
熟記這些單字

8 come from   出生於；來自；從……取得結論；由……引起

- My best friend Bill **comes from** Chicago.
  我最好的朋友比爾來自芝加哥。

- Where did all these hats **come from**?
  這些帽子是哪裡來的？

- If you ask me, the best cherries **come from** Washington.
  如果你問我，我會說最好吃的櫻桃來自華盛頓。

9 every other (one)   每隔……

- Terrance visits his uncle and aunt **every other** week.
  泰倫斯每隔週都會去拜訪叔叔和阿姨。

10 mix up 使混亂；搞混

- It's easy to **mix up** Richie and Lou because they're twins.
  瑞奇和盧是雙胞胎，所以很容易把他們搞混。

- I always **mix** your birthday **up** with Seth's.
  我老是把你和塞斯的生日搞混。

mix up the twin babies
把雙胞胎嬰兒搞混

mix up the photos
弄亂相片

11 make out 辨別出；理解；填寫；試圖證明；成功辦到

- The TV volume was so low that it was hard to **make out** what the actors were saying.
  電視的音量很小，實在很難聽出演員在說什麼。

make a check out
開支票

make out the meaning of the words
理解文字意思

Waiting for a Friend
等朋友 🎧 031

Jaime is waiting for Marc under an apple tree.
Finally, he arrives—15 minutes late.
潔咪在蘋果樹下等馬克，終於，他出現了，在遲到了 15 分鐘後。

Jaime: Hey, Marc! Why are you late?
What have you **been up to**[1]?

Marc: Sorry! I had a hard day at school. Can we talk about it for a minute? This morning, my professor seemed to **find fault with**[2] everything I said during class. He wanted me to totally **do my report over**[3]. Really, he seemed to **be carried away**[4] with new ideas, and his thoughts were hard to **keep track of**[5].

Jaime: Don't worry! You'll **get through**[6] it; it's only a paper!

Marc: I guess you're right. But **from now on**[7], I think I'd better try being a better student. Hey, did you bring any food in that bag? I'm hungry.

Jaime: **Keep away from**[8] my bag! There's a surprise in there for you—but you have to wait. I don't want you to see it yet.

潔咪：　嘿，馬克，你為什麼遲到？你**都在做**什麼呢？

馬克：　對不起，我今天在學校過得很不愉快，我們可以聊一下嗎？今天早上教授對我在課堂上的發言好像很**有意見**，他要我**重寫**報告。真的，他似乎**被**新的思想**影響**，很難**猜測**他在想什麼。

潔咪：　別擔心！你**寫**得**完**的，不過是報告而已！

馬克：　妳說得對，但是我想我**今後**最好試著當個好學生。嘿，那個袋子裡頭有吃的嗎？我餓昏了。

潔咪：　**別靠近**我的袋子！裡面是要給你的驚喜，但是你必須等等，我還不想給你看。

find fault with 挑毛病

keep away 遠離

032

1 be up to
正在做某事；由……決定；
做壞事（違法的事情）

- What **are** you **up to** this weekend?
  你這週末要做什麼？

- I don't know if we'll play video games tonight; it's **up to** you.
  我不知道今晚是否要打電動，由你決定。

- I'm sure Walt **is up to** something; he's been acting so strangely lately.
  我確定華特一定在做什麼見不得人的事情，他最近的行為很奇怪。

2 find fault with 挑毛病；找碴

- George is so critical; no matter how good things are, he always **finds fault with** something.
  喬治很吹毛求疵；就算東西再好，他也能夠挑出毛病。

3 do over 重做

- My math teacher said I could **do** the last quiz **over** because I did so poorly on it.
  因為我考得很差，所以數學老師說我可以重考上次的小考。

4 be carried away 開心到忘我的境界

- Tina likes baking so much that she **was carried away** and made hundreds of cookies.
  堤娜熱愛烘焙到忘我的境界，她不小心做了一堆餅乾。

- Harry **was** so **carried away** by the good news that he couldn't calm down.
  哈利沉醉在好消息中，無法冷靜下來。

- People in the crowd **were carried away** by Clinton's passionate speech.
  觀眾因柯林頓滿腔熱血的演講而興奮不已。

5 keep track of 追蹤；密切注意

- Agatha is always traveling, and I can never **keep track of** where she is.

  雅嘉薩老是在旅行，所以我永遠無法掌握她的行蹤。

- The babysitter is supposed to **keep track of** my little sister.

  保姆應該要隨時注意我的妹妹。

6 get through 完成；通過；聯絡上

- Please leave Jimmy alone; he won't **get through** his work if you keep chatting with him.

  請不要煩吉米，你一直和他聊天，他無法完成工作。

- Jimmy **got through** his exams without too much trouble.

  吉米輕輕鬆鬆地通過了考試。

- I tried to phone her, but I couldn't **get through**.

  我試著打電話給她，但是聯絡不上。

7 from now on 從今以後

- **From now on**, you must be home before midnight.

  從今以後，你必須在午夜前回家。

- Because I overslept again, I have to work the late shift **from now on**.

  由於我又睡過頭，從現在開始我必須上晚班。

- **From now on**, the gates will be locked at midnight.

  從現在開始，大門半夜都會上鎖。

033

8 keep away (from) 遠離;不許靠近

- Danielle is just a child, so be sure to **keep** her **away from** the road.
  丹妮葉拉還是個小孩,所以千萬別讓她靠近馬路。

- I suggest you **keep away from** Jane; she has a cold.
  我建議你別靠近珍,她感冒了。

- **Keep away from** the edge of the cliff. 別太靠近懸崖。

9 look into 調查;研究

- Vince was **looking into** the possibility of working in Canada.
  文斯正在研究到加拿大工作的可能性。

- I'm not sure if that's a good price for that car; let me **look into** it.
  我不確定那是那台車最好的價錢,讓我研究一下。

- They're **looking into** the possibility of merging the two departments.
  他們正在研究合併兩個部門的可能性。

10 take hold of 抓住

- The boy **took hold of** his mother's hand before they crossed the street.
  男孩在過馬路前抓住媽媽的手。

- When they got to the city center, Patty **took hold of** her camera and didn't let go because she was afraid it would get stolen.
  他們進入市中心後,派蒂怕相機被偷,所以緊抓著不放。

11   ill at ease   緊張；不安

- As he was waiting for the test results, Carl felt **ill at ease**.
  卡爾在等待考試成績時感到緊張。

12   keep out   不許進入；避免捲入某種情況

- I want some privacy now, so please **keep out** of my room.
  我現在想要有一點隱私，所以請不要進入我的房間。

- If you see two people arguing, it's best to **keep out** of it.
  如果你看到兩個人在爭吵，最好別被牽扯進去。

The New Mobile Phone
新手機 (034)

Josh tells Abby about his new mobile phone.
喬許把新手機的事情告訴艾比。

Abby: Wow! Is that your new cell phone?

Josh: You bet. Cool, isn't it? My old one was really **out-of-date**[1].

Abby: Well, this one sure is **up-to-date**[2]. But I thought your old phone worked fine.

Josh: Actually, I really needed this one. Last weekend, the old charger **caught fire**[3] when I plugged it in. Good thing it happened when I was around; otherwise, I might have **burned down**[4] the apartment building!

Abby: Okay, so it **stands to reason**[5] that you needed a new phone—but what made you choose this model?

Josh: I think it looks cool! **As for**[6] the old phone, I gave it to my friend.

艾比： 哇，那是你的新手機嗎？

喬許： 沒錯，很棒吧？我的舊手機真的**過時**了。

艾比： 嗯，這支確實**很新**。但我以為你的舊手機還可以用。

喬許： 事實上，我真的需要換支新的了。我上週末使用舊的充電器時，竟然**著火**了。好險我當時在，否則整棟公寓可能會**燒掉**！

艾比： 嗯，所以你**理所當然**需要新手機，但你為何會選擇這個款式呢？

喬許： 我覺得它很好看！**至於**舊手機，我送給朋友了。

Cassettes are now out-of-date.

錄音帶現在已經過時了。

1 out-of-date 過時的

- This computer is so **out-of-date** that it can't even connect to the Internet.
  這台電腦很老舊了，就連網路也無法連接。

- Cassettes and even CDs are now **out-of-date** because everyone uses MP3s.
  錄音帶甚至 CD 現在都過時了，大家都在用 MP3。

2 up-to-date 擁有最新資訊；現代的

- If you want to work as a reporter, you really must keep yourself **up-to-date** on current events.
  如果你想成為記者，就必須隨時掌握最新消息。

- A good fashion designer stays **up-to-date** on the newest styles and trends.
  優秀的服裝設計師總是能夠掌握最新的流行款式和趨勢。

- This new laptop player is really **up-to-date**—it's a new model.
  這台新的筆記型電腦確實是最新的，它是全新的機種。

- Keep your boss **up-to-date** on your progress.
  隨時向你的老闆報告最新進度。

3 catch fire 著火

- Despite being wet, the wood that they put on the stove finally **caught fire**.
  儘管他們放在火爐上的木頭是濕的，它們最後還是燃燒了起來。

catch fire 著火

- If you don't move that candle away from the curtains, they may **catch fire**.
  如果你不把蠟燭從窗簾移走，窗簾可能會著火。

4 burn down 燒毀；燒成灰燼

- Fortunately, the Stern family had fire insurance, so when their house **burned down**, they were able to buy a new one.

  幸好史坦一家有火災保險，所以他們的房子燒掉後，他們能買新房子。

- Don't ever light matches in my house. I'm afraid you'll accidentally **burn** it **down.**

  不要在我家點火柴，我很怕你不小心會把房子燒掉。

burn down 燒毀

5 stand to reason 合理的；自然

- If you never brush your teeth, it **stands to reason** that you'll spend a lot of money at the dentist's office.

  如果你從不刷牙，花很多錢看牙醫是很合理的。

- It **stands to reason** that students who study the hardest get the best grades.

  用功的學生成績較好，這是理所當然的。

6 as for 關於

- **As for** Bill, he ended up writing a book and becoming famous.

  至於比爾，他最後因寫了一本書而變得很有名。

- Today is a beautiful day; **as for** tomorrow, however, we can expect rain.

  今天天氣晴朗。至於明天，可能會下雨。

7 **burn up** 燒光；使發怒

- The photographs in Ray's bedroom were **burned up** in the fire.
  雷房間的那場大火，燒光了他的照片。

- The bad news really **burned** him **up**.
  那個壞消息真的令他很生氣。

8 **burn out** 使筋疲力盡；（機器）燒壞；燒盡

- In his last year of high school, Louis **burned out** and got terrible grades.
  路易在高中的最後一年累壞了，所以成績很糟糕。

- The writer **burned** himself **out** as he finished his first book.
  作者完成了第一本書後便累壞了。

- After she used the old laptop for six hours straight, it **burned out** and wouldn't turn on anymore.
  那台舊筆記型電腦在她使用了整整六個鐘頭後便燒壞，再也無法開機了。

9 **blow up** 使爆炸；使勃然大怒；使（氣球、輪胎）膨脹；使（照片）放大

- The best part of the action movie was when the gas tank **blew up** and started a huge fire.
  這部動作片最精采的部分就是油箱爆炸而引發大火了。

- My dad **blew up** when he saw the phone bill.
  我爸爸看到電話帳單後氣炸了。

10 break out 使爆炸;使勃然大怒;使(氣球、輪胎)膨脹;使(照片)放大

- Irma and Gina got more and more angry with each other, and it wasn't long before an argument **broke out** between them.
  由於娥瑪和吉娜越來越生對方的氣,於是他們之間的爭吵爆發了。

- When Damian returned from school, his mother saw that he had **broken out** with chicken pox.
  當戴明恩從學校返家後,媽媽發現他突然長了水痘。

- In the news today I saw that three thieves **broke out** of jail!
  我在今天的新聞上看到有三位小偷逃獄了!

11 feel sorry for 深表同情

- I **felt sorry for** Matilda when I heard she was kicked out of her apartment.
  當我聽到瑪蒂蓮達被趕出公寓時,我對她深表同情。

- Seeing that poor bird in the little cage really made me **feel sorry for** it.
  我很同情那隻被關在小籠子裡可憐的鳥兒。

12 make good 成功;實現承諾

- Linda **made good** on her decision to study economics.
  琳達實現了決定讀經濟學的承諾。

- Brad **made good** on his promise to study more and get better grades.
  布萊德實踐了他會更用功以取得好成績的承諾。

make good 成功

- She was described as the local girl who **made** it **good** in Hollywood.
  她代表了在好萊塢大放光彩的鄉村女孩。

73

13

Walking Along the Beach
海邊散步 🎧 1037

Jolene and Charlie are talking while taking a walk along the beach. 裘琳和查理在海邊一邊聊天一邊散步。

Charlie: You know, it's **once in a blue moon**[1] that we have this kind of weather in the spring. It's perfect for taking a walk on the beach! It's something we shouldn't **take for granted**[2].

Jolene: You're right, Charlie, especially if we **take into account**[3] that usually it's raining this time of year. Things really **turned out**[4] well.

Charlie: Hmm, maybe it'll rain after all. Let's go back. Taking a walk on the beach this time of year really **calls for**[5] umbrellas.

Jolene: You **give up**[6] too easily! A little rain never hurt anyone.

Once in a blue moon, a woman gives birth to triplets.
很少有女人能生出三胞胎。

查理： 唉，我們**很少**能在春天有這樣的天氣，到海邊散步正好！
我們不應該**認為**這是稀鬆平常的。

裘琳： 你說的沒錯，查理，尤其是**考慮到**現在已經是春天了，每
年這個時間通常都在下雨。天氣能**變成**這樣真好。

查理： 嗯，可能快要下雨了。我們回去吧。每年此時到海邊散步
真**需要**帶把傘。

裘琳： 你太容易就這麼**放棄**了！這種毛毛雨不會有影響的。

take into account 考慮

give up 放棄

038

1 once in a blue moon 很少；不常

- Amy's brother is always traveling, so they see each other only **once in a blue moon**.
  艾咪的哥哥一直都在旅行，所以他們很少見面。

- **Once in a blue moon,** a woman gives birth to triplets.
  很少有女人能生出三胞胎。

- My cousin lives in Philadelphia, so I get to see him only **once in a blue moon**.
  我的表弟住在費城，所以我不常和他見面。

2 take for granted 將……視為理所當然；不重視；想當然

- Sheila helps her brother a lot, but sometimes she feels **taken for granted**.
  席拉幫了她哥哥很多忙，但她有時感覺不被重視。

- Only after her computer broke did she realize how much she **took** having a laptop **for granted**.
  她在電腦壞掉後，才知道她忽視了電腦的重要性。

- Many people **take** it **for granted** that the future will be better.
  許多人都認為未來會更美好。

- So many of us **take** clean water **for granted**.
  許多人都把乾淨的水視為理所當然。

3 take into account 加以考慮

- Even if you don't do well on this test, the teacher is sure to **take** your good attitude and hard work **into account** when she gives you your final grade.
  就算你這次考不好，老師在打總成績前，會把你良好的學習態度和努力列入考慮的。

- Beth had planned to write her research paper over the weekend, but she forgot to **take into account** the fact that the library would be closed then.
  貝絲計畫在週末寫研究報告，但她沒有考慮到週末圖書館不開放。

4 turn out
結果是；出席；生產（產品）；關掉

- As things **turned out**, it was a good idea to go on vacation last month.
  事情證明了上個月去度假是一個好主意。

- When the president gave a speech in Central Park, thousands of people **turned out**.
  總統在中央公園發表演說，有上千名民眾前往參加。

- They **turn out** thousands of shoes every week.
  他們每個星期生產好幾千雙鞋子。

5 call for
需要；要求；接某人

- Wow, a toothache like that definitely **calls for** a dentist.
  哇，牙齒痛成那樣絕對需要看牙醫。

- When Tommy couldn't finish the project on his own, he **called for** help.
  當湯米無法自己完成這項企劃，他要求支援。

6 give up
放棄

- Don't ever **give up**; just keep trying.
  永遠不要放棄，要不斷嘗試。

- I know things look difficult now, but don't **give up** on your dreams; if you work hard enough, things may get better.
  我知道事情現在看起來很難，但別放棄你的夢想。只要你夠努力，情況就會好轉。

- Starting next week, Felix plans to **give up** smoking.
  菲力斯計畫從下星期開始戒菸。

039

7 make clear 使清楚明白

- Ronald really didn't **make clear** what time we were supposed to show up.
  羅納多並沒有清楚說明我們應該何時出席。

- Dr. McCormack **made** it perfectly **clear** that you were supposed to come to work early today.
  麥科馬克醫師清楚交代過，你今天應該要提早來上班。

8 come to 恢復意識；合計

- It took Amy a few hours to **come to** after the operation.
  艾咪在手術過後幾個小時才恢復意識。

- Has she **come to** yet? 她恢復意識了嗎？

- With tax, your bill **comes to** $450.24.
  加上稅金後，您的帳單總共是 450.24 元。

9 break down （機器）故障；崩潰；衰退；腐敗

- Just as we were driving away from the house, our car **broke down**.
  我們正要開車離家時，車子壞了。

break down 故障

78

10 have on 穿戴（衣服、首飾、鞋子）

- Gary's wife was angry with him when she saw that he didn't **have** his wedding ring **on**.
  蓋瑞的太太發現蓋瑞沒戴婚戒時，
  她很生氣。

- Carol didn't want to answer the door because she **had on** only a bathrobe.
  卡蘿不想開門，因為她身上只穿著浴袍。

have on a bathrobe 穿著浴袍

11 cross out 畫線刪除

- The teacher **crossed out** a lot of my text and told me to write those parts over.
  老師把許多我寫的字劃掉了，還要我把那些部分重寫。

- It was hard to see who the letter was from because someone had **crossed out** the return address.
  有人把回信地址劃掉了，所以很難看出信是誰寄的。

ACTION!
~~TALK~~

Babysitting
照顧小孩 🎧 ⟨040⟩

Sam and Nancy have a chat.
山姆和南西在聊天。

Sam: What are you doing tonight?

Nancy: I have to **look after**[1] my little cousin Billy while his parents are **eating out**[2].

Sam: You have a cousin named Billy? I've never **heard of**[3] him.

Nancy: That's because his family lives in Ontario, Canada. They're visiting my mom for a few weeks.

Sam: Are you **looking forward to**[4] spending time with your cousin?

Nancy: **As a matter of fact**[5], it won't be fun at all. Billy always **has his way**[6], so he is really poorly behaved.

Sam: Oh, sorry to hear that. Do you have to do this? Maybe your uncle and aunt can find someone else to take care of him.

Nancy: I have no choice; it's **cut-and-dried**[7]. But I'll **hear from**[8] my aunt as soon as they're on their way home. If you **feel like**[9] it, we can see a movie afterward.

Sam: Good idea!

山姆： 妳今晚要做什麼呢？

南西： 我必須**照顧**我的表弟比利，他的父母今晚要**在外面吃飯**。

山姆： 妳有個表弟叫做比利？我怎麼從來沒**聽說**過他。

南西： 因為他們家住在加拿大安大略省。他們這幾個禮拜是來探望我媽媽。

山姆： 妳**期待**和你的表弟一起玩嗎？

南西： **其實**，那一點也不好玩。比利總是**為所欲為**，他是一個不聽話的孩子。

山姆： 噢，真遺憾。妳一定要照顧他嗎？也許你的叔叔和阿姨可以找其他人幫忙照顧他？

南西： 我別無選擇，這是**事先安排**好的事情。但在他們回來的路上，我阿姨會**通知**我。如果你**想要**的話，我們之後可以去看場電影。

山姆： 好主意！

041

1   look after   照顧

- When my folks are at work, I **look after** my little sister.
  父母去上班時,我要照顧我妹妹。

- Who **looks after** your dog when you are in class?
  你去上課的時候,誰來照顧你的狗?

- I **look after** the neighbors' cat while they're away.
  鄰居不在的時候,我替他們照顧貓咪。

2   eat out   在餐廳用餐

- There's nothing good to eat at home, so let's **eat out** for dinner.
  家裡沒有什麼好吃的東西,所以我們到外面吃飯。

- When I lived in Seattle, I used to **eat out** all the time.
  我住在西雅圖的時候,都在外面吃飯。

3   hear of   聽說;得知;考慮

- Before my trip to Africa, I had never **heard of** Madagascar.
  到非洲旅遊前,我從沒聽說過馬達加斯加島。

- There are many classical musicians whom I've never **heard of**.
  有許多古典音樂家我都沒有聽過。

- Damien wanted to go out with his friends Wednesday night, but his mother wouldn't **hear of** it because he had school the next day.
  戴明恩星期三晚上想要和朋友出去,但他媽媽因為隔天要上課所以不同意。

4 look forward to 期待；盼望

- I always **look forward to** three-day weekends because I am able to do some traveling.
  我總是盼望著一連三天的週末到來，那樣我就可以出外旅遊。

- My little brother is **looking forward to** his birthday party.
  我的小弟期待著生日派對的到來。

5 as a matter of fact 事實上

- **As a matter of fact**, Martin recently graduated from college.
  事實上，馬汀最近大學畢業了。

- Cindy just got a new TV, **as a matter of fact**.
  事實上，辛蒂才剛買了一台新的電視。

6 have one's way 照某人的意思去做；為所欲為

- Sometimes it feels like I never **have my way**.
  我有時覺得天從人願。

- Because Carol is the youngest child, she always **has her way**.
  卡蘿是家中的么女，所以她好像老是為所欲為。

7 cut-and-dried 可預期的；明確的

- After the discussion, the CEO reached a **cut-and-dried** decision.
  討論結束後，執行長得到了一個預料中的結論。

- The choices we make in life are rarely as **cut-and-dried** as we would like.
  我們在人生中所做的選擇，通常是無法預期的。

042

8   hear from   接到某人的消息

- I hope Ray is okay. I haven't **heard from** him since he arrived in the United Kingdom.
  我希望雷沒事。自從他去了英國，我就沒了他的消息。

- Teresa expects to **hear from** Samuel next week.
  泰瑞莎盼望下星期能接到山姆爾的消息。

9   feel like   想要做某事

- Do you **feel like** going to the movies tonight?
  你今晚想要看電影嗎？

- I don't **feel like** going out for Chinese food; my stomach hurts.
  我今晚不想出去吃中國菜，我胃痛。

10   once and for all   一勞永逸地

- As soon as Jared stapled the pages of his report together, he knew he was done with it **once and for all**.
  傑瑞德把報告裝訂好後，便了解到他終於把它完成了。

11 make fun of 嘲笑

- Diane's new suit was so unusual that it was hard not to **make fun of** her.

  黛安新買的套裝很奇怪，令人很難不去取笑她。

12 come true 實現；成真

- Although Warren always dreamed of buying a Ferrari, he never thought the dream would **come true**.

  雖然華倫常常幻想能買一輛法拉利，但他從沒想過會實現。

- The party was everything I had hoped for; it was as if all my wishes **had come true**.

  這個派對就是我想要的，假如我的願望都能成真的話。

- The good things we've been hoping for are actually **coming true**.

  我們一直期望的好事真的實現了。

| Raul and Emily gossip about school life.
勞爾和艾蜜莉在討論學校生活的八卦。

Emily: Did you hear what happened with the teacher who is **filling in**[1] for Ms. Santos today?

Raul: No. What happened?

Emily: She arrived for her first day of teaching with her shirt **inside out**[2]!

Raul: Ha, ha, ha! That's funny! Is she a good teacher at least?

Emily: Yeah, she's ok. First she made us **fill out**[3] some forms, and while we were doing that, she left for a few minutes. Some people started making jokes and talking. When she came back, she was mad.

Raul: What did she say?

Emily: She said that she is **in touch**[4] with Ms. Santos, and if we don't behave, she'll **take** this problem **up with**[5] her personally.

Raul: It may be tempting for the students to **take advantage of**[6] the situation now, but **in the long run**[7], it isn't a good idea. Ms. Santos isn't a forgiving person!

艾蜜莉： 你聽說今天**代替**山托斯女士的那位老師所發生的事情了嗎？

勞爾： 沒有，怎麼了？

艾蜜莉： 她第一天代課就把襯衫**穿反**了！

勞爾： 哈哈哈！真好笑！至少她是個好老師吧？

艾蜜莉： 是啊，她還不錯。她一開始要我們**填寫**一些表格，我們在填的時候，她離開了一下子。有些人便開始講話和開玩笑，所以她回來後就生氣了。

勞爾： 那她說了些什麼？

艾蜜莉： 她說她有**和**山托斯女士**聯絡**，如果我們表現不好，她會當面**和**她**商量**。

勞爾： 現在這種情形其實**對**學生很**有利**，但**長遠來看**並不是一個好主意。山托斯女士並不是一個性情溫和的人！

take up with 與某人商量某事

fill in 代替

87

044

1 fill in 填寫；代替

- The directions on the test were to **fill in** the spaces with the correct answers.
  作答方式為在試卷上的空格填入正確答案。

- I'm not his regular secretary—I'm just **filling in**.
  我並不是他固定的秘書，我只是來代班的。

2 inside out 內外反過來；徹底地

- How embarrassing it was to arrive at school with my pants **inside out**.
  我到學校才發現把褲子穿反了，真糗。

- She had her sweater on **inside out**. 她把毛衣穿反了。

3 fill out 填寫；增胖

- If you want to apply for a passport, you have to **fill out** many forms.
  如果你想申請護照，必須要填寫許多表格。

- All students must **fill** this document **out** before taking the SAT.
  所有參加 SAT 考試的學生都必須先填寫這份文件。

fill out 填寫

- Her figure began to **fill out** once she started college.
  她上大學後便開始增胖了。

4 in touch （透過電話、信件、電子郵件或其他方式）和某人聯絡

- Katherine and I have been **in touch** since high school.
  我和凱瑟琳從高中到現在一直都有聯絡。

- I want to keep **in touch** with you even after I move away.
  我就算搬家也想和你聯絡。

in touch 和某人聯絡

5 take up with 與某人商量某事

- I think it's time to **take up** the issue of a raise **with** my boss.
  我想我該和老闆商量加薪的事情了。

- If you don't like the policy, **take** it **up with** the manager.
  如果你不喜歡這項政策，就和經理商量。

6 take advantage of 善用；乘人之危

- Suzanna **took advantage of** the gym on campus and worked out every day.
  蘇珊娜善用學校的健身房，她每天都去健身。

- I think he **takes advantage of** her good nature.
  我覺得他在利用她善良的本性。

- I thought Francesca was nice until I saw how she **took advantage of** Dale and made him do all her work. 在我發現法蘭西絲卡利用戴爾替她完成所有的工作前，我一直以為她是個好人。

045

7   in the long run 從長遠來看；一段時間後

- You may not like the idea of getting braces, but **in the long run**, it is the right thing to do.

  你也許不喜歡戴矯正器，但久了以後你會發現這麼做是正確的。

- Buying these baby kittens may seem like a good idea now, but **in the long run**, it may be a mistake.

  買小貓現在看來是一個好主意，但一段時間後你可能會覺得這是個錯誤。

8   take after 長得很像（通常指親戚）

- Everyone tells me I **take after** my father because we are both tall and have red hair.

  每個人都說我和父親長得很像，因為我們都很高，也都有一頭紅髮。

- Francine really **takes after** her older brother; they have such similar interests.

  法蘭欣和她哥哥真的長得很像，他們的興趣也很相近。

- Most of my children **take after** my wife, both in appearance and character.

  我孩子的外貌和個性都和我太太很像。

- Tina **takes after** her mother's side of the family.

  緹娜和她媽媽那邊的親戚長得很像。

take after 長得很像

9   **no matter** 無論；縱使

- I don't want to take any calls, **no matter** who it is.
  我不想接任何電話，不管誰打來都一樣。

- We'll definitely play basketball this weekend, **no matter** what the weather; we'll play even if it is raining!
  無論天氣如何，我們這週末一定會去打籃球，就算下雨也會去打球！

My Note

The New Neighbor

新鄰居 🎧 046

Tommy and Adrian talk about a new neighbor.
湯米和雅德恩在討論新鄰居。

Tommy: How are you getting along with your new neighbor, Mr. Dasey, these days?

Adrian: Well, to be honest, things aren't as bad as before. Although we don't always **see eye to eye**[1], we've been **making the best of**[2] things.

Tommy: That's good. **For once**[3], there doesn't seem to be any serious problem between you two.

Adrian: I **keep in mind**[4] that Mr. Dasey is an old man and that he's **hard of hearing**[5], so sometimes he doesn't understand everything I say. The only problem now is that he keeps the TV on very loud because of his hearing problems.

Tommy: I bet you'd like it if his TV suddenly **went off**[6] and never came back on.

Adrian: I'm not that mean!

湯米： 妳這幾天和妳的新鄰居戴西先生相處得如何？

雅德恩： 嗯，老實告訴你，比以前好多了。雖然我們的**看法**常常不**相同**，不過我們都**盡力**了。

湯米： 那很好啊。**至少這次**你們兩個之間沒什麼嚴重的問題。

雅德恩： 我會**記住**戴西先生是一個老人家，而且有**重聽**，所以有時會聽不懂我說的話。現在唯一的問題就是，由於他聽力很差，因此老是把電視開得很大聲。

湯米： 我相信你一定想要他的電視會突然**壞掉**，而且修不好。

雅德恩： 我沒那麼壞心！

see eye to eye 看法相同

hard of hearing 重聽

047

1 see eye to eye 看法一致

- Although Beth and I don't get along, we definitely **see eye to eye** on a lot of political issues.

  雖然我和貝絲處不來，但我們的政治理念許多都是一致的。

- As a teenager, Vic never **saw eye to eye** with his parents.

  維克是青少年，所以他和父母從未有過一致的看法。

2 make the best of 充分利用

- Although it rained the entire time, we decided to **make the best of** our camping trip and went fishing and hiking.

  這次露營雖然一直在下雨，我們還是決定把握機會去釣魚和健行。

- Whenever something goes wrong, Hector tries to **make the best of** it.

  無論發生什麼事情，赫克托總是全力以赴。

3 for once 僅這一次

- **For once**, Darren arrived to class on time.

  戴倫就這麼一次準時到學校上課。

4 keep in mind 記住

- Before you go out to the party this weekend, **keep in mind** that there is an exam on Monday .

  在你週末去參加派對前，記住星期一要考試。

- When you are making dinner, you must **keep in mind** that Anne's brother doesn't eat meat.

  你在準備晚餐時，要記住安的哥哥不吃肉。

5 hard of hearing 重聽的

- When Erin's grandmother watches TV, she has to turn the volume way up because she is **hard of hearing**.

  因為艾琳的奶奶重聽，所以她看電視時必須把音量轉很大聲。

- My father is quite old now, and he's increasingly **hard of hearing**.

  我的父親年紀大了，重聽也越來越嚴重了。

6 go off 機器停止；離開；警報響起；爆炸；發生；變糟；食物壞掉

- During the thunderstorm, all the lights in the house suddenly **went off**.

  暴風雨來臨時，屋內突然停電了。

- I think Janet **went off** to the market a few minutes ago.

  我想珍娜幾分鐘前才剛離開到市場去了。

- The alarm on Dean's wristwatch **goes off** every day at lunch.

  狄恩手錶上的鬧鐘每天午餐時間都會響。

- The bomb **went off** at midnight.

  炸彈在半夜的時候爆炸。

- The protest march **went off** peacefully with only two arrests.

  示威遊行在和平中進行，只有兩個人被逮捕。

- That paper has really **gone off** since they got that new editor.

  那家報社自從聘請了那位新編輯後，品質就變得很糟糕。

048

7 cut off 切斷；剪短；中斷（電話、有線電視、網路）

- Nina **cut off** the top of the carrots before cooking them.

  妮娜在煮紅蘿蔔前先去頭。

- When Todd stopped paying his bills, the company **cut off** his Internet connection so he couldn't go online anymore.

  陶德停付帳單後，電信公司便中斷了他的網路，所以他再也不能上網了。

cut off 切斷

8 cut out 剪下；停止

- Nelly **cut** her ex-boyfriend **out** of all the photos she had of them.

  奈莉把所有前男友的照片都剪掉。

- Phillip, will you **cut** that **out**! I can't study if you're making noise.

  菲力普，你能停止嗎！你這麼吵我沒辦法唸書。

cut out 剪下

9 get along 有進展；處理；生存

- It's hard **getting along** in a new city.
  在陌生的城市中很難生存。

10 grow out of 因長大而不適合（衣服、鞋子）；產生於；因長大而戒除

- The new mother didn't want to spend too much money on shoes for her baby because she knew he'd **grow out of** them quickly.
  新手媽媽不想要花太多錢買寶寶的鞋子，因為她知道他長大後很快就會穿不下。

11 on one's toes 保持警覺的

- Having twins really keeps my mom **on her toes**.
  有雙胞胎小孩真的讓我媽變得非常小心。

My Note

The Surprise Party
驚喜派對 [049]

| Rob and Gale discuss a surprise party.
| 羅伯和格兒在討論一場驚喜派對。

Gale: It's funny to think that just two days ago, I was convinced that celebrating my birthday was a **lost cause**[1].

Rob: What do you mean?

Gale: Well, I had invited my friends over, but they all **turned** me **down**[2].

Rob: That's terrible!

Gale: It was! Then, as my dad and I were **shutting up**[3] his shop last night, I heard some strange noises.

Rob: Oh! Was someone **breaking in**[4]?

Gale: No, it was a surprise party! My dad and my friends were there with a cake, so I made a wish and **blew out**[5] the candles.

Rob: That sounds like a big shock; **above all**[6], it sounds like you had a great time!

格兒： 現在回想起來很好笑，兩天前我還覺得不可能要辦成一場很棒的派對已經是**不可能**的事情了。

羅伯： 什麼意思？

格兒： 唔，我之前邀請了我的朋友，但他們全都**拒絕**了我。

羅伯： 真糟糕！

格兒： 本來很糟！然而，昨晚我和我老爸在**關**店時，我聽到一些奇怪的聲音。

羅伯： 噢！有人**闖進去**了嗎？

格兒： 不，那是個驚喜派對！我爸和我朋友都在那裡，還有一個蛋糕，所以我許了一個願望，然後把蠟燭**吹熄**。

羅伯： 聽起來像是個超級大驚喜。**最重要的是**，妳似乎度過了一段很愉快的時光！

turn down 拒絕　　　break in 闖入

99

1 lost cause 敗局已定;毫無希望

- I tutored Jan every day for a few months, but when I realized it was a **lost cause**, I gave up.
  我每天教珍功課已經好幾個月了,但當我發現毫無幫助時便放棄了。

- Arnold practiced the trumpet every day for three months, but finally he decided it was a **lost cause** and sold it.
  阿諾三個月來每天練習吹喇叭,但最後他認為沒有希望便把它賣掉了。

- Gina has already made up her mind, and it's a **lost cause** to try to change it.
  吉娜已經下定決心了,想要使她改變心意是不可能的。

2 turn down 拒絕;降低(電視、收音機的)音量、亮度

- When Mike asked Barbra to the dance, she **turned** him **down**.
  當麥可邀請芭芭拉跳舞時,她拒絕了他。

- Ryan **turned down** the job because it involved too much traveling.
  萊恩因為這份工作需要常出差,所以拒絕了。

- Please **turn down** the volume on the computer; I can't concentrate when you are playing video games.
  請把電腦的音量轉小,你打電動會讓我無法專心。

3 shut up 關閉(英式用法);閉嘴(不禮貌的用法)

- Before leaving for the night, the manager **shut up** the shop.
  經理晚上離開前把店門關上。(英式用法)

- Please **shut up**! I'm trying to study.
  請閉嘴!我正要試著唸書。

4 break in 闖入；打斷談話；使用後逐漸適合

- Ralph was shocked to find that someone had **broken in** and stolen his laptop.

  瑞夫發現有人闖入，並且偷走他的筆記型電腦時，他很震驚。

- Fran **broke in** on the conversation and asked my name.

  法蘭打斷了談話並問了我的名字。

5 blow out 吹熄（蠟燭）；（輪胎）爆裂

- Steve took a deep breath and **blew out** all the candles on his birthday cake.

  史帝夫做了一個深呼吸，然後把生日蛋糕上所有的蠟燭都吹熄了。

- Richie lit a cigarette and quickly **blew** the match **out**.

  瑞奇點燃香菸後，立刻把火柴吹熄。

blow out candles
吹熄蠟燭

6 above all 特別；尤其

- Mindy is a nice girl—she's hard-working, clever, and **above all**, honest.

  敏蒂是個好女孩，她做事認真、聰明，最重要的是，她很誠實。

- She loved swimming and jogging; but **above all**, she loved her family.

  她熱愛游泳和慢跑，但最重要的是，她愛她的家人。

7   become of 發生

- After she moved to Egypt, Aunt Sarah stopped sending letters, and no one knew what **became of** her.

  莎拉阿姨自從搬到埃及後便不再來信，所以沒人知道她發生了什麼事。

- I'm not sure that we'll ever know what **became of** my cat after it ran away.

  我的貓不見後，我不確定我們是否能知道牠發生了什麼事。

8   have got   擁有；持有

- I **have gotten** a new bicycle, and I am riding it every day.

  我得到一台新腳踏車，而且我每天都會騎它。

- What **have** you **got** in
  your bag?

  你的包包裡有什麼？

have got 擁有

9   have got to 必須

- I **have got to** get to class now, or I'll be in trouble.

  我現在必須去上課，不然會有麻煩。

- Frank **has got to** leave the party before 8, or he'll miss his bus home.

  法蘭克必須在八點前離開派對，否則他會錯過回家的公車。

10 keep up with 不落後於；跟上

- Terrance walks so fast, it's hard to **keep up with** him sometimes.

  泰倫斯走路很快，有時候要跟上他的腳步很難。

11 on the other hand 另一方面；相對地

- That car looks so cool, but **on the other hand**, it is very expensive.

  那台車看起來真酷，但另一方面，它也很貴。

- I was happy we bought a new flat screen TV, but **on the other hand**, it was so big I didn't know where we would put it.

  我很高興我們買了一台平面電視，但另一方面，因為它很大台，所以我不知道要把它擺在哪裡。

Finding a Lost Dog
尋狗啟示 🎧052

Sally and Mohammed talk about a lost dog.
莎莉和穆罕默德在談論走丟的狗狗。

Sally: Have you seen my dog, Rex? I've been looking for him all day.

Mohammed: No, but **according to**[1] my neighbor, there was a dog digging in our garden earlier.

Sally: That **is bound to**[2] be Rex!

Mohammed: How did he get away, anyway?

Sally: Well, when we **ran out of**[3] dog food, my mom sent me to the store to buy some more. I opened the door and **was about to**[4] go out when Rex just ran away.

Mohammed: Oh man! Let's go to my house and see if he's around there.

Sally: I hope so. It'll feel nice to **tear up**[5] all these "Lost Dog" signs once I get Rex back.

莎莉： 你有看到我的狗狗雷克斯嗎？我已經找他找了一整天了。

穆罕默德： 沒有，但**根據**鄰居的說法，之前有隻狗在我家院子裡挖洞。

莎莉： 那**肯定**是雷克斯！

穆罕默德： 反正他是怎麼不見的？

莎莉： 就是我們家的狗飼料**沒**了，我媽要我去商店買。我**正好**打開門要出去，雷克斯就跑了出去。

穆罕默德： 噢，天啊！來我家看他是否還在那裡吧。

莎莉： 希望他還在。一旦找到了雷克斯，就可以開開心心地把這些尋狗啟示給**撕掉**了。

tear up 撕掉

run out of 用完

1 **according to** 根據;據……所記載

- **According to** many scientists, it will be possible to live on Mars one day.
  根據多位科學家的說法,人類也許有一天能夠居住在火星上。

- You've spelled the word incorrectly **according to** the dictionary.
  根據字典上所寫,你拼錯字了。

2 **be bound to** 可能(肯定)會發生

- With all the traffic tonight, Craig **is bound to** arrive late.
  今晚大塞車,克雷格鐵定會遲到。

3 **run out of** 用完

- So many people came to our restaurant yesterday that we **ran out of** eggs.
  昨晚餐廳的生意很好,
  所以我們的雞蛋都用完了。

- When Gina's grandpa **ran out of** coffee, he sent her to the store to buy more.
  吉娜的爺爺喝完咖啡後,
  便要吉娜到商店再多買一些。

4 **be about to** 正好;準備要

- I **was about to** call my girlfriend when she knocked on my door.
  我女朋友敲我的房門時,我正好要打電話給她。

- Diane **is about to** have her first baby.
  黛安就快要生第一胎了。

5   tear up   撕毀

- When Florence got an "F" on her essay, she **tore** it **up** before her mom could see it.

  佛羅倫絲的作文得到了「F」，所以她在媽媽看到前就先撕掉了。

- After Eric broke up with his girlfriend, he **tore up** all the love letters she had sent him.

  艾瑞克和女朋友分手後，他把所有她寫的情書都撕掉了。

6   tear down   拆除

- The family **tore down** some of the old walls before adding a new room to the house.

  這戶人家在蓋新房間前，把一些舊的牆拆掉。

- Because the tree house seemed unsafe for the children, Mr. Grey **tore** it **down**.

  對孩子來說，樹屋好像很不安全，所以蓋瑞先生把它拆掉了。

7   at heart   實際上；內心是

- Although Mr. Williams may act grumpy, he's a good guy **at heart**.

  雖然威廉斯先生性情乖戾，然而他實際上是個好人。

- No matter how much bad news I read, I still believe that most people are good **at heart**.

  無論看了多少不好的新聞，我還是相信人其實都是善良的。

8 for sure 肯定；確定地

- Jessica will win the race **for sure**; she's a fast runner.
  潔西卡肯定會贏得比賽，她跑得很快。

- We're coming to visit you **for sure** this weekend.
  我們這星期肯定會去拜訪你的。

9 go over 被接納；仔細檢視；複習

- Mr. Belvedere's first class was long and boring, so it didn't **go over** very well.
  貝維德雷先生的第一堂課既漫長又無趣，因此不太被接受。

- Let's **go over** the article one more time before the test.
  我們在考試前再把文章仔細看一遍吧。

go over 複習

10 take for 誤以為

- After Roxanne made a big mistake, some teachers **took** her **for** a fool; however, she's very clever.
  在羅姍妮犯下大錯後，有些老師把她當傻瓜，但其實她非常聰明。

- Do you **take** me **for** a fool?
  你以為我是傻瓜嗎？

- I **took** her **for** Mrs. White.
  我把她誤認為懷特太太。

11　try out　試用

- Before you buy a new scooter, you should **try** it **out** to make sure you like it.
  買新摩托車前最好要先試騎，以便確定你是真的喜歡。

- Do you want to **try out** my new digital camera?
  你想要試用看看我新買的數位相機嗎？

- Don't forget to **try out** the equipment before setting up the experiment.
  開始實驗前別忘了先測試一下儀器。

12　do without　沒有⋯⋯而將就；過著沒有⋯⋯的日子

- When Brenda lost her job, the family had to learn to **do without** many luxuries.
  布蘭達丟了工作後，她的家人必須要學會放棄許多奢侈品。

- While spending the summer in China, Bill had to **do without** some of his favorite foods.
  比爾在中國度過夏天時，必須要放棄他最愛的食物。

Applying to a University
申請大學 🎧055

Leo and Catherine talk about applying to a university.
里歐和凱瑟琳在討論申請大學的事情。

Leo: So, did you get any university acceptance letters yet?

Catherine: No, I didn't. I'm afraid **putting up with**[1] all the boring applications that the guidance counselor **passed out**[2] and comparing all the different programs was **in vain**[3].

Leo: You haven't received any replies yet? Oh man! I bet that is all you think about **day in and day out**[4].

Catherine: You better believe it! I've applied to so many colleges, I can't **tell** their names **apart**[5].

Leo: Maybe you should have focused on just two or three schools and put more effort into the applications.

Catherine: I suppose so. **All in all**[6], I should have thought about this more carefully.

里歐：	妳接到任何一所大學的入學許可了嗎？
凱瑟琳：	沒有。我**受不了**指導老師**發**的無聊申請書，還有**白費力氣**比較所有不同的課程。
里歐：	妳還沒收到回覆嗎？ 噢，老天！我打賭你一定**每天**都在想這件事情。
凱瑟琳：	沒錯！我申請了好幾間大學，但**分不清楚**它們的名字。
里歐：	也許妳應該專心申請兩、三家學校就好，然後多做點努力。
凱瑟琳：	我想也是。**總之**，我應該再仔細想一想。

pass out 分發   tell the twins apart 辨別雙胞胎

056

1 put up with 忍耐

- When Rich moved near the highway, he had a hard time **putting up with** the noise.
  瑞奇搬到公路附近後，他無法忍受噪音。

- After a long, tough day at school, it is sometimes hard to **put up with** my little sister.
  在學校度過了既漫長又艱難的一天後，我有時會無法忍受我妹妹。

2 pass out 分配；昏厥

- Please **pass out** these forms to everyone who comes to the meeting.
  請把這些表格發給所有出席這次會議的人。

- The professor asked Mindy to **pass out** a test to each student.
  教授要敏蒂把考卷發給每一位學生。

- When a baseball hit Martha in the head during the game, she **passed out** for a few minutes.
  馬莎在比賽中被棒球打到，昏過去好幾分鐘了。

pass out 昏厥

3 in vain 白費

- Two weeks of constant studying were **in vain** as Mabel got a "D" on her chemistry exam.
  美貝的化學考試得到「D」，她連續唸了兩個禮拜的書都白費了。

- Francis tried **in vain** to arrive on time to her first class of the semester.
  法蘭西絲為準時上這學期第一堂課所做的努力都白費了。

4   day in and day out 每天

- The traffic to New York City is terrible **day in and day out**.
  往紐約市區的交通每天都很亂。

5   tell apart   區別

- The teacher had a hard time **telling** the twins **apart**.
  老師不太能夠辨別雙胞胎。

- Can you **tell** these two kittens **apart**?
  你可以分辨出這兩隻小貓嗎？

6   all in all   整體而言

- Despite the fact that the car broke down, **all in all** it was a fun day.
  儘管車子壞了，整體而言，今天依然是愉快的一天。

- **All in all**, this is a very interesting class.
  大致說來，這堂課非常有趣。

- **All in all**, I think we can say the visit was a success.
  整體而言，我認為這次訪問非常成功。

7   be in (the/one's) way 阻礙；造成不便

- The only annoying thing about having a puppy is that he **is** always **in the way**.
  養狗最擾人的就是不方便。

- You're **in the way**; please give me some space!
  你妨礙到我了，請給我一些空間！

057

8   bite off   咬斷

- Your dog **bit off** a piece of my Christmas decoration.
你的狗咬掉了我的耶誕裝飾。

- Felix **bit off** a piece of the chocolate bar and threw the rest away because it tasted terrible.
因為巧克力棒很難吃，菲力斯咬了一塊後便把剩下的都丟掉。

9   catch up   追上

- He was out of school for a while and is finding it hard to **catch up**.
他一陣子沒去學校上課，所以很難趕上進度。

10   go around   四處走動；流傳；足夠分配

- At the picnic, there were hardly enough sandwiches to **go around**.
三明治根本不夠分給野餐的每個人。

- Let's **go around** the lake on our walk; it looks so peaceful.
我們今天就在這座湖的四周逛逛吧，這裡看起來一片祥和。

go around 四處走走

11   put on   增加（如體重）

- When Clarence returned from visiting his family for the summer, he had **put on** a few pounds.
克萊倫斯自從夏天探望家人回來後，他的體重便增加了好幾磅。

12 put up 提供住宿；舉起；建設

- When Carl visited Chicago, I **put** him **up** in my apartment.
  卡爾來芝加哥玩時，我安排他住在我的公寓。

- Vicky **put** the painting **up** above the fireplace.
  薇琪把畫舉起來，掛在火爐上方。

- Did you know that they're **putting up** a new cafe next to the supermarket?
  你知道他們要在超市旁邊蓋一家咖啡廳嗎？

put up 建設

Finding a Lost Cat

尋貓啟示 [058]

Ivy and Andy talk about a funny incident with a cat.
艾薇和安迪在討論一個有關貓咪的有趣意外。

Ivy: What's **the matter**[1]? You look exhausted.

Andy: I took the cat in for his first visit to the vet, and he just couldn't **hold still**[2]. It was annoying!

Ivy: What happened? Did he run away?

Andy: Yes, he did! The vet said this was the craziest cat he's ever seen, **by far**[3].

Ivy: Well, **no wonder**[4]! It sounds like your dear cat was pretty mad! I hope he hasn't **gotten lost**[5].

Andy: Don't worry, I'll find him; I **know** him **by sight**[6].

Ivy: Get going! I'll **see** you **off**[7] right now. And remember to look everywhere; don't **rule out**[8] any possible hiding places.

hold still 不動

艾薇：　　**怎麼了**？你看起來累壞了。

安迪：　　我第一次帶我的貓去看獸醫，可是他就是不能**不動**。很討厭！

艾薇：　　發生了什麼事情？他跑走了嗎？

安迪：　　沒錯，他跑了！獸醫說他**顯然**是他所看過最難馴服的貓。

艾薇：　　嗯，也**難怪了**！聽起來你的貓不太聽話！希望他別**迷路**才好。

安迪：　　別擔心，我會找到他的，我**認得**他。

艾薇：　　快點開始找吧！我現在就**送**你**離開**。記得每個地方都要找，別**漏掉**任何地方。

run away
離家出走；逃跑

get lost 迷路

117

1 be the matter 傷腦筋；出狀況

- Are you okay, or **is** something **the matter**?
  你沒事吧？還是哪裡不舒服嗎？

2 hold still 不要動

- Amy is only 3 years old, so it is hard for her to **hold still** when she visits the dentist.
  艾咪才三歲，所以看牙醫時很難要她不要動。

- **Hold still**; this won't hurt.
  不要亂動，不會痛的。

3 by far 遠高於；顯然

- This weekend in Venice was one of the best weekends of my life, **by far**.
  這次在威尼斯度週末顯然是我這輩子最棒的週末之一。

- This lesson is, **by far**, one of the most boring I've ever seen.
  這堂課顯然是我上過最無聊的課之一。

4 no wonder 難怪

- **No wonder** you're tired; you were up till 3 a.m. last night!
  難怪你累了，你昨晚熬夜到凌晨三點！

- **No wonder** I couldn't find my keys! They were in the car all along.
  難怪我找不到鑰匙！原來一直都在車上。

5   get lost   迷路

- It was Dan's first time visiting
  San Francisco, so it's no surprise
  that he **got lost**.
  這是丹第一次到舊金山，
  所以他會迷路一點也不令人意外。

- I **got lost** in the London
  Underground yesterday.
  我昨天在倫敦地鐵站迷了路。

6   know by sight   認得

- I'm not sure of Gina's address, but I **know** the house
  by sight.
  我不確定吉娜家的地址，但我認得她的房子。

- Although Carla has never spoken with Will, she
  knows him **by sight**.
  雖然卡拉從未和威爾說過話，但她認得他。

7   see off   （幫某人）送行

- When my uncle Chip was leaving, the whole family
  went with him to the airport to **see** him **off**.
  我叔叔奇普要離開時，我們全家人陪他到機場為他送行。

- I'd like to go to lunch with you tomorrow, but I have
  to **see off** my friend who is traveling to Bermuda.
  我明天想和你吃中餐，但我必須為要去百慕達的朋友送行。

- My parents **saw** me **off** at the airport.
  我父母到機場為我送行。

- Families gathered at the dock to **see** the sailors **off**.
  家人聚集在碼頭邊為船員們送行。

8   rule out   使成為不可能；排除可能性；不予考慮

- The constant rain **ruled out** Sophia's plans to go sunbathing.
  外頭一直下雨，蘇菲亞做日光浴的計畫泡湯了。

- Because mom **ruled out** my plans to get a pet snake, I decided to ask her for a pet spider.
  既然媽媽不考慮讓我養寵物蛇，我決定要求她讓我養寵物蜘蛛。

9   see out   送某人到門口；持續到結束

- After dinner, we **saw** Ben **out** the front door.
  晚餐後，我們送班到前門口。

- It is polite to **see** your guests **out** after they visit.
  送來訪的客人到門口是一種禮貌。

see out 送某人到門口

10   hold up   拖延；搶劫

- Because my mother was stuck in traffic, the family meeting was **held up**.
  我媽媽遇上塞車，因此家庭聚會延後了。

- Derek's delayed flight **held** the workshop **up**.
  由於戴瑞克的班機延誤，所以研討會延後了。

11 run away 離家出走；逃跑

run away 逃跑

- Last week my dog **ran away**, and I haven't seen him since.
  自從上星期我的狗跑掉後，我就沒再見過他。

- When the children heard the loud bang of the fireworks, they got scared and **ran away**.
  小朋友聽到巨大的煙火聲後，都被嚇跑了。

12 bring up 養育（小孩、動物）；提出議題

- Gary **brought up** his five children by himself.
  蓋瑞獨自扶養五個小孩。

- Some of the students **brought** questions **up** with the teacher after class.
  下課後，有些學生向老師提出問題。

- They **brought** him **up** as a Christian.
  他們將他養育成為基督教徒。

bring up questions 提出議題

bring up children 養育小孩

Handing in a Paper
交報告 🎧 [061]

Francine and Albert talk about the deadline for their papers.
法蘭欣和艾伯特在談論有關報告的截止日期。

Francine: Did you finish your research paper? You know you have to **hand** it **in**[1] today.

Albert: I was up all night checking it over **in case**[2] I made some mistakes. I don't want to be **taken by surprise**[3] with a bad grade.

Francine: Good job! I'm nearly done too. However, as soon as class starts, I'm going to **go up to**[4] the professor and ask him a few questions.

Albert: It may be a bit late for that. You'd better try to finish now. Trust me, you'll **be better off**[5] that way.

Francine: You know, Albert, that's a good idea. You're smart! I bet you're **named after**[6] Albert Einstein!

法蘭欣： 你的研究報告寫完了嗎？你知道今天一定要**交**吧。

艾伯特： 為了**以防**錯誤，我昨晚整夜沒睡仔細檢查了一遍。我可不想看到成績時**嚇一跳**。

法蘭欣： 做得好！ 我也快要寫完了，只要一開始上課，我便會**走過去**問教授一些問題。

艾伯特： 那可能有點太遲了吧。妳最好現在就完成。相信我，我覺得那樣會**比較好**。

法蘭欣： 艾伯特，這主意不錯。你真聰明！我想你的名字是以艾柏特·愛因斯坦來**命名**的吧！

hand in 繳交　　　　be taken by surprise 嚇一跳

062

1   hand in   繳交；提出

- Ms. Applebee told us we had to **hand in** our reports by next week.
  艾波比女士說我們下星期前一定要交報告。

- Did you **hand** your essay **in** yet? 你交論文了嗎？

- I've decided to **hand in** my resignation.
  我已經決定要遞出辭職信了。

- The teacher told the children to **hand in** their exercise books.
  老師要孩子們繳交練習簿。

2   in case   假使；以防萬一

- You should take your umbrella to work today **in case** it rains.
  你今天最好帶把傘去上班，以防下雨。

- **In case** of emergency, remember that you can always call my cell phone.
  如果有任何緊急狀況，記得要打手機給我。

- I don't think I'll need any money, but I'll bring some just **in case**.
  我不認為我會需要用到錢，但我會帶著以防萬一。

- Bring a map **in case** you get lost.
  把地圖帶著，免得你迷路了。

3 take by surprise 感到意外；撞見

- Mohammed's new haircut really **took** me **by surprise**; I hardly recognized him!
  穆罕默德的新髮型讓我很意外，我幾乎認不出他來了！

- I was **taken by surprise** with your mobile's new ringtone—it is very original!
  我對你的手機鈴聲感到很意外，真有創意！

- Lisa's resignation **took** us completely **by surprise**.
  莉莎的辭呈令所有人感到相當地意外。

4 go up to 接近

- Bill told his little sister never to **go up to** strangers.
  比爾告訴妹妹不要接近陌生人。

- Irene **went up to** the next person she passed on the street and asked for directions.
  艾琳走向迎面而來的路人問路。

- Let's **go up to** the second floor of the restaurant to eat because there are more tables there.
  我們到這家餐廳的二樓吃東西吧，樓上的座位比較多。

5 be better off 比較好的狀況

- After a few months in driving school, Victoria **was better off** on the roads.
  維多莉亞到駕訓班上了幾個月的課後，她的開車技術好多了。

- We **were better off** once we got off the plane and got some fresh air.
  我們在下了飛機、呼吸到新鮮的空氣後，便感覺好多了。

- He'd **be better off** working for a bigger company.
  他在大公司工作的話大概會比較有錢。

063

6 name after 以……來命名

- Harriet is **named after** her grandmother.
  哈莉特是以其祖母的名字來命名。

7 hold on 稍等；抓緊；堅持下去

- **Hold on**, I'll be with you in a minute.
  請您稍等一下，我馬上就回來。

- The receptionist asked us to **hold on** for a while because there were many visitors in the office.
  由於辦公室有許多訪客，所以接待員請我們稍等一下。

- **Hold on** to your hat when the wind is blowing, or it will blow away!
  起風時要抓緊你的帽子，
  否則會被吹走！

hold on 稍等

- If you can **hold on**,
  I'll go and get some help.
  如果你能夠在那裡等一下，
  我會過去，並且找人幫忙。

8 take apart 拆開

- If you **take** the computer **apart**,
  you may end up breaking it.
  如果你把電腦拆開，最後可能會
  把它弄壞。

126

9   pull together 同心協力

- Everyone in the office **pulled together** to finish the project.

  這份企劃案是由公司上上下下每個人共同合力完成的。

- If we want to meet the deadline, everyone has to **pull together** and work all night.

  如果我們想要趕上截止日期，就必須同心協力，熬夜趕工。

- Everyone on our street really **pulled together** after the fire.

  火災發生後，街上的人全都團結在一起。

10   keep in touch with 和某人保持聯絡

- Although Rachel moved away from home, she **keeps in touch with** her family by calling every week.

  雖然瑞秋離家了，但她依然每個禮拜打電話和家人保持聯絡。

- Karin bought a new cell phone so she could **keep in touch with** her friends more easily.

  卡琳買了一支新手機，
  以便她和朋友保持聯絡。

The New Teacher
新老師 🎧 064

Molly and Philip have a chat about their new teacher.
茉莉和菲利普在聊他們新來的老師。

Molly: How do you like our new history teacher?

Philip: Well, after hearing that he studied at Harvard, I really **look up to**[1] him; but the fact is, he seems to **look down on**[2] his students.

Molly: Yeah, he may be a smart guy, but he's not so friendly. Yesterday I **came across**[3] him in a café, and though I **took pains**[4] to be nice, he was pretty cold.

Philip: I know what you mean. I **stopped by**[5] his office a little while ago with some questions, and he wasn't very helpful.

Molly: Nope. The last teacher was better; he even told us to **drop** him **a line**[6] by email if we had any questions about the assignments.

Philip: Exactly. Plus, this class seems harder—I don't think I **stand a chance**[7] of getting an "A."

茉莉： 你喜歡新來的歷史老師嗎？

菲利普： 唔，自從知道他是哈佛畢業的，我便很**尊敬**他，但事實上，他似乎有點**瞧不起**學生。

茉莉： 是啊，他博學多聞，但不是很友善。我昨天在咖啡店**巧遇**他，雖然我**努力**釋出善意，但他看來很冷漠。

菲利普： 我懂你的意思。我前一陣子**到**辦公室請教他一些問題，但他不是很樂意幫忙。

茉莉： 沒錯，之前的老師比較好，他甚至說如果我們有課業方面的問題，隨時可以用電郵**寫信**給他。

菲利普： 是啊，加上課程越來越難了，我不認為我**有希望**得到「A」。

drop a line 寫信　　　look down on 瞧不起

1 look up to 尊敬

- Ariel **looks up to** her older sister.
  艾芮兒很尊敬她姐姐。

- Whom do you **look up to** most?
  你最尊敬的人是誰？

- Judy was older and more experienced, and I **looked up to** her.
  裘蒂年紀較長，經驗較豐富，我很尊敬她。

2 look down on 瞧不起

- A good boss doesn't **look down on** his employees.
  好老闆不會看不起員工。

- Sometimes I feel as if my professor is **looking down on** me because I got a "D-" on the exam.
  自從考試得到「D-」後，我有時覺得教授看不起我。

3 come across 被認為是；突然遇見或發現

- Mariah **comes across** really well on television.
  瑪莉亞在銀光幕前的形象很好。

- Although Melinda is a nice girl, she can **come across** as a bit mean sometimes.
  記住，就算瑪琳達是個好女孩，她有時也是很難相處的。

4 take pains 不辭辛勞；費盡苦心

- Adriana **took pains** to walk quietly so as not to awaken the baby.

  艾卓恩娜努力走路不發出聲音，以免吵醒小寶寶。

- Dan **took** great **pains** to eat right so he would lose weight.

  丹為了減輕體重，很努力養成正確的飲食習慣。

5 stop by 暫訪

- If you have time tomorrow, **stop by** in the afternoon.

  明天如果有空，就下午過來吧。

- **Stop by** on your way home, and I'll give you that DVD.

  回家路上順便到我這裡來一下，我要拿那片 DVD 給你。

6 drop (someone) a line 打電話給某人；寫便條給某人

- This weekend, I'll **drop** my friend Jerry **a line** if I have time.

  如果有時間，我這週末會寫信給我的朋友傑瑞。

- I would have **dropped** you **a line** earlier, but I lost your address.

  我之前本來要寫信給你，但我弄丟了你的地址。

- I really do like hearing from you, so **drop** me **a line** and let me know how you are.

  我真的很想知道你的消息，
  寫封信給我，讓我知道你的近況。

7 stand a chance 有機會；有希望

- Matilda isn't a very good swimmer; she doesn't **stand a chance** of winning the gold medal.
  瑪蒂蓮達游得不快，她沒什麼希望贏得金牌。

- Rory's mom is mad at her, so she doesn't **stand a chance** of going to the movies with us this weekend.
  蘿芮的媽媽在生蘿芮的氣，所以她這週末不可能會和我們去看電影了。

8 stand for 忍受；支持；代表

- Don't use foul language with me; I won't **stand for** that kind of talk.
  和我講話別用粗話，我無法忍受那種說話方式。

- The stars on the U.S. flag **stand for** states.
  美國國旗上的星星代表各州。

9 take off （飛機）起飛；突然受到歡迎

- Because of the snowstorm, no planes **were taking off** or landing at the airport.
  由於暴風雪的因素，機場所有的飛機都無法起降。

take off 飛機起飛

- Her singing career had just begun to **take off**.
  她的歌唱事業才剛爆紅。

10 look on 觀看;把……視為

- Because Toby arrived at the airport late, he could only **look on** as the plane left without him.
  陶比太晚到機場,所以他別無選擇只能眼看著飛機離開。

- Janet had a broken leg, so she could only **look on** as the other students played soccer.
  珍娜自從腿骨折後,就只能看著其他學生踢足球。

11 keep time (鐘錶的時間)精準;計時

- This old clock doesn't **keep** good **time**.
  這個老舊的時鐘不準。

- Does your cell phone **keep time**?
  你手機的時鐘準嗎?

- When I go running, I like to **keep time** on my watch.
  慢跑時,我喜歡用手錶來計時。

keep time 精準

12 pull off 拉掉;成功辦到

- I **pulled off** my wet clothes as soon as I got home.
  我一到家就趕緊脫掉濕衣服。

- It was a hard exam, but in the end I **pulled** it **off** and got an "A."
  考試很難,但我還是成功地得到「A」。

- Although no one thought he could do it, Corey **pulled off** the best business deal in company history.
  雖然沒有人認為柯瑞能夠成功,
  但他談成了公司有史以來最好的一筆交易。

pull/take off 脫掉

The Weekend Party
週末派對 🎧 |067|

Zack and Ursula talk about Ursula's party.
查克和娥蘇拉在討論娥蘇拉的派對。

Zack: How did your party go last weekend?

Ursula: Bad. I worked so hard to make it nice. I **cleaned out**[1] all the shelves and cabinets and washed all the dishes; I really did my best to **make do**[2] with my small apartment.

Zack: Did your roommates **go in for**[3] the idea of a party?

Ursula: At first, my roommates **got on my nerves**[4] when they **put down**[5] the idea of a party. However, when I told them that their friends could come too, they almost **took over**[6] the party planning.

Zack: So what went wrong? It sounds good so far.

Ursula: I **stayed up**[7] the entire night before to make sure all the details were right. The next day, I **stayed in**[8] waiting for the guests. I didn't go to work; I didn't study. I just waited.

Zack: And?

Ursula: No one **showed up**[9]!

查克： 上週末的派對辦得如何？

娥蘇拉： 糟透了。我非常努力想讓一切看起來都很棒，我把床鋪下面都**清理乾淨**了，也把所有的盤子都洗乾淨了。我真的**盡力**把公寓整理乾淨了。

查克： 妳的室友們**喜歡**辦派對這點子嗎？

娥蘇拉： 他們剛開始**批評**這個想法時**讓我很緊張**，但我說他們的朋友也可以來參加後，他們幾乎**接手**計畫了整個派對。

查克： 那是哪裡出了錯？到目前為止聽起來都很好啊。

娥蘇拉： 我為了確認所有細節都沒錯，前一天晚上**熬夜**沒睡。隔天我**在家**等候客人的光臨，沒去上班，也沒唸書，我只是等待。

查克： 然後呢？

娥蘇拉： 都沒有人**來**！

clean out 清理乾淨

stay up 熬夜

135

068

1   clean out   清理乾淨

- The fridge smelled terrible, so Damian **cleaned out** all the old food.
  冰箱的味道很臭，所以戴明恩把過期食物都清理乾淨。

- Someone better **clean out** the garage soon; it is filling up with junk.
  車庫堆滿了垃圾，最好盡快把它清理乾淨。

2   make do   將就

- After Mindy quit her job, she had to **make do** with less.
  敏蒂辭職後，必須依存較少的物資得過且過。

3   go in for   參加比賽；喜歡；把……當作興趣

- All Scotts coworkers **went in for** the idea of having a surprise party for his retirement.
  史考特所有的同事都參與了為他舉辦退休驚喜派對的計畫。

- Abe doesn't **go in for** baseball, but he sometimes watches his friends play.
  艾比不喜歡棒球，但他有時會去看朋友打球。

4   get on one's nerves   令人心煩或討厭

- My neighbor's dog really **gets on my nerves** when he barks all night.
  鄰居的狗叫了整晚，令我心浮氣躁。

- After spending so much time together on the cruise, Jan and Gary **got on each other's nerves**.
  珍和蓋瑞自從一起參加郵輪之旅後便很討厭對方。

5 put down 放下；奚落；鎮壓

- It was very embarrassing when my brother **put** me **down** in front of all my friends.
  我的哥哥在所有朋友面前奚落我，令我很難堪。

- The dictator used the army to **put down** the democratic rebellion.
  獨裁者用武力鎮壓民主反抗團體。

put down 奚落

6 take over 接管；帶至某處

- When the CEO was in the hospital, his assistant **took over** the company for a few weeks.
  執行長住院時，他的助理接管了公司好幾個星期。

- After the rebellion, a new leader **took** the country **over**.
  叛亂結束後，新的領導者接管了整個國家。

- The delivery boy **took** the package **over** to my aunt.
  送貨員把包裹交給我阿姨。

- Richard has **taken over** responsibility for this project.
  理查已經接手負責整個企劃。

069

7   stay up   熬夜

- The children get to **stay up** all night on New Year's Eve.

  孩子們除夕夜可以整晚不睡覺。

- How late did you **stay up** last night? You look very tired.

  你昨晚熬夜到幾點？你看起來很累。

8   stay in   待在家

- Although Ralph planned to go to a club, he ended up **staying in** and watching a movie on TV.

  瑞夫雖然計畫要去俱樂部，但他最後待在家裡看電影。

- Instead of going to a restaurant, let's **stay in** and make dinner here.

  我們待在家裡自己做晚餐，別上館子了。

9 show up 到達；出現

- Unfortunately, we **showed up** at the movie a few minutes late, so we missed the beginning.
  可惜我們電影開演了幾分鐘才進場，所以錯過了開頭。

- I invited her for eight o'clock, but she didn't **show up** until eight-thirty.
  我約她八點見面，
  但她一直到八點半才出現。

10 close call 千鈞一髮；倖免於難

- I almost didn't get into the university; my test scores were barely high enough, so it was a **close call**.
  我差一點就上不了大學，我的考試成績勉強夠高，真是千鈞一髮。

- I really had a **close call** today on the way home from school—I almost drove off the icy road!
  我今天放學回家真的差點就發生意外，我的車子在結冰的路上打滑，差點就駛出車道。

11 give birth to 生孩子

- Our rabbit **gave birth to** seven baby bunnies last weekend!
  我們養的兔子上週末生了七隻小兔子！

139

Schoolwork Problems
課業問題 🎧070

Walt is telling Debby about some problems in his class.
華特告訴黛比他上課遇到的一些問題。

Debby: Is everything ok? You look like you need to **cheer up**[1].

Walt: Well, I **ran into**[2] some problems with my schoolwork in philosophy.

Debby: What happened? Are you having trouble doing what you **set out to**[3] do in that class?

Walt: Bingo. I just can't finish this report. I'm even thinking about **dropping out of**[4] this philosophy class.

Debby: That's so extreme that it doesn't even really **make sense**[5]. If I were you, I'd **draw up**[6] a list of goals you need to **carry out**[7] and then complete them one by one.

Walt: But I set out to finish this report by next week!

Debby: Relax, I **believe in**[8] you. Just don't give up, and everything will be okay, I'm sure.

黛比： 一切還好嗎？看來你需要**振作**一下。

華特： 唉，我在寫哲學作業時**遇到**一些問題。

黛比： 怎麼了？你在**準備**做那堂課的作業時遇到困難了嗎？

華特： 沒錯。這份報告我就是寫不完。我甚至考慮**退掉**這門哲學課。

黛比： 太誇張了，那樣做一點**意義**也沒有。如果我是你，我會**擬訂**一張要**達成**目標的清單，然後一項一項去完成。

華特： 但我打算下星期前要完成這份報告耶！

黛比： 放輕鬆，我**相信**你。只要別放棄，我確定一切都會很順利的。

cheer up 振作

draw up a list 擬定清單

1 cheer up 使高興；使生動

- When Gary was sick in bed for a month, his friend visited him dressed in a funny costume to try and **cheer** him **up**.

  蓋瑞在病床上躺了一個月，為了讓他開心，朋友去探望他時穿了很滑稽的服裝。

- A coat of paint and new curtains would really **cheer** the kitchen **up**.

  新的窗簾和油漆讓廚房完全明亮了起來。

2 run into 偶遇；撞上

- We **ran into** a lot of traffic on the way to the airport.

  我們在前往機場的路上遇上塞車。

- Jack **ran into** Betty at the supermarket; it was the first time he had seen her in years.

  傑克在超市偶遇貝蒂，這是他多年來第一次看到她。

run into 偶遇

3　set out to　開始做；有計畫地做

- Ryan **set out to** write the perfect college application letter. 雷恩打算寫一份最理想的大學推薦信。

- What will you **set out to** do after graduation? 你大學畢業後計畫做什麼？

- Although we **set out to** buy some milk and eggs, we ended up buying a new laptop. 雖然我們計畫要買一些牛奶和雞蛋，但最後我們卻買了一台新的筆記型電腦。

4　drop out of　退出；脫離

- After breaking his leg, Will **dropped out of** the race. 威爾腿骨折後便退出了比賽。

- When the judges discovered that Tracy had copied her artwork from another painting, they made her **drop out of** the competition. 當評審發現崔西的作品是模仿別幅畫時，便要她退出比賽。

5　make sense　有邏輯；合乎道理的

- If you didn't do the homework, the teacher's lecture will not **make sense**. 你如果不做功課，會聽不懂老師教的。

- This assignment is hard; I don't think it **makes** any **sense**. 這份作業很困難，我不認為這是合理的。

6　draw up　制定；草擬

- The lawyer **drew up** a document putting Calvin in charge of his elderly mother's affairs. 律師擬定了一份文件，指定凱文負責照顧年邁母親的生活起居。

- Felix **drew** a list **up** so that he could plan his week better. 菲力斯擬定了一張週計畫表以便做規劃。

7 **carry out** 開始執行；實踐

- The students were told to **carry out** every task their teacher expected of them.
  老師期望學生能完成所有的任務。

- I know you have a plan, but I hope you have time this weekend to **carry** it **out**.
  我知道你有計畫，但我希望你有時間在這週末完成。

8 **believe in** 相信；相信……的存在（通常指幽靈或宗教信仰）

- Although Rachel failed a few classes this semester, I **believe in** her; I think she'll be successful.
  雖然瑞秋這學期有幾門課被當掉，但我還是相信她。我認為她會成功的。

- Patty doesn't **believe in** ghosts.
  派蒂不相信幽靈的存在。

9 **meet** (someone) **halfway** 與人妥協

- Diane wanted to be paid $500 for her translation, and I wanted to pay her only $250. In the end, we **met** each other **halfway** and agreed on $375.
  黛安想要我付她 500 元的翻譯費用，而我只想付她 250 元，我們最後以 375 元妥協。

- Just when it seemed that the negotiations would never end, Jane found a way to **meet halfway** and lowered the price of the minivan.
  看來協商會沒完沒了，珍於是發現降低小卡車的售價是一種妥協的方法。

10 give-and-take 相互退讓

- Good business practices require a level of **give-and-take**.

  想要完成一筆愉快的交易，包括一定程度的相互妥協。

- Happy family relations require **give-and-take**, I think.

  我認為家庭的和諧需要相互讓步。

- They reached an agreement after many hours of bargaining and **give-and-take**.

  經過了好幾個小時的協商和退讓後，他們終於達成了協議。

- In every friendship, there has to be some **give-and-take**.

  每一段友情中都會需要相互退讓。

11 knock out 擊倒；使昏迷；使筋疲力盡；摧毀

- Phil fell off his bike and **knocked** himself **out**.

  菲爾從腳踏車上摔下來後昏倒了。

- The doctor warned me that this painkiller might **knock** me **out**.

  醫生警告我，服用這種止痛藥可能會感到疲倦。

- The sleeping tablets **knocked** me **out** for 18 hours.

  安眠藥讓我昏睡了 18 個小時。

Cheating on a Test
考試作弊 🎧 073

Diane and Pete have a chat about a recent test.
黛安和彼得在聊最近的考試。

Diane: I can't believe you **got away with**[1] cheating on the test.

Pete: Well, it was tough. I think the girl next to me knew what I was doing, but she didn't **let on**[2]. If she did, I'm sure things would have **gone wrong**[3].

Diane: Lucky for you that you don't **stand out**[4] as the kind of person who would cheat.

Pete: Right. It's a good thing that the teacher never **checked up on**[5] me too carefully.

Diane: Well, if you ask me, getting caught would **serve you right**[6].

Pete: Hey! How else can I **keep up with**[7] this class?

Diane: Try studying like the rest of us!

黛安： 我不敢相信你考試作弊竟然還能**逃過一劫**。

彼得： 是啊，這件事實在很棘手。我想隔壁的女生知道我在做什麼，但她沒有**洩漏**出去。如果她說了，我想事情一定會**變得很嚴重**。

黛安： 幸好你不像那些會作弊的人那麼**引人注目**。

彼得： 是啊，老師從來不會仔細**檢查**我，真好。

黛安： 唔，我認為啊，你**活該**被抓。

彼得： 嘿！否則我如何才能**趕上**班上的程度呢？

黛安： 就和我們其他人一樣讀書啊！

let to 洩漏（祕密）

147

1 get away with 成功地逃過懲罰

- Mindy **got away with** stealing strawberries from her neighbor's garden; nobody ever caught her.
  敏蒂在鄰居家的院子裡偷摘草莓，僥倖地逃過一劫，至今還沒有人抓到她。

- Nobody **gets away with** cheating in this class.
  這個班上從來沒有人能夠作弊而不受到懲罰。

2 let on 洩漏（秘密）

- I suspect Sally knows more about this than she's **letting on**.
  我懷疑莎莉知道的比她所透露的還要多。

- I tried not to **let on** that I knew the answer.
  我試著不透露其實我已經知道答案。

3 go wrong 情況不順利；弄錯

- Every detail about the trip to the seaside had been carefully planned, so we believed nothing could **go wrong**. And then it poured.
  海邊之旅的所有細節都經過詳細的規劃，因此我們相信事情很順利，不過後來卻下了傾盆大雨。

- After studying for a week, Amanda was confident about the test; she was sure nothing would **go wrong**.
  亞曼達唸了一整個星期的書，所以對考試很有信心，她確信一切會很順利。

- I thought I had done this correctly; I can't understand where I **went wrong**.
  我以為這件事情我做對了，我不知道究竟是哪裡出了錯。

4 stand out 引人注目；優秀傑出

- Donald never dressed conservatively like his colleagues, and the bright colors he wore really made him **stand out** in a crowd.

  唐諾的穿著不像同事那麼保守，因此穿著鮮豔的他在人群中非常引人注目。

- It **stands out** as an excellent school among many very good schools.

  在許多好學校中，它顯然是一所聲譽極佳的學校。

- We had lots of good applicants for the job, but one **stood out** from the rest. 這個職位有許多條件不錯的人選，但其中一位應徵者在所有人當中脫穎而出。

- His bright red hair helps him **stand out** at comedy clubs.

  他那亮紅色的頭髮是他在喜劇俱樂部引人注目的原因。

stand out 脫穎而出；引人注目

5 check up on 調查；探望某人或聯絡某人以確定某人安好

- Derek's mother called him at summer camp to **check up on** him.

  戴瑞克的母親打電話到夏令營找戴瑞克，以確定他安然無恙。

6   serve (someone) right 某人應得的懲罰

- Because Lucas delayed the flight by coming late, everyone onboard thought that losing his first-class seat **served** him **right**.

  由於盧卡斯遲到使得班機延誤，所以機上所有人都認為他活該喪失頭等艙的位子。

- It **serves** Marla **right** that she got an "F" in class because she never studied.

  因為瑪拉從不唸書，所以她活該得到「F」。

7   keep up with 與……保持聯繫；趕上

- Because Alfred missed a few weeks of class, he had a hard time **keeping up with** his classmates.

  亞佛烈德好幾個星期沒去上課，他為了趕上同學的進度所以很辛苦。

- My grandmother doesn't **keep up with** new products—she's never even heard of a DVD player.

  我外婆不太能跟上流行，她甚至沒聽說過 DVD 播放器。

8   keep up 持續（某種情況）；使保持清醒

- If you **keep up** the good work, there's no question that you'll get an "A" in this class.

  你如果繼續保持好成績，這堂課肯定能得到「A」。

- Wow, you're doing great work; be sure to **keep** it **up**!

  哇，你做得很好，一定要繼續保持！

9　**burst out**　突然大笑、大哭；大聲地喊

- "Come back!" Marc **burst out** as his girlfriend walked away.

  馬克的女朋友離去時，他大聲地喊：「回來！」

burst out 大聲地喊

10　**stick up**　伸直；突出；持槍行搶或被搶

- Some large rocks were **sticking up** out of the water.

  有一些巨大的石頭伸出在水面上。

- When Betsy wakes up in the morning, her hair is always **sticking up**.

  貝西早上起床時，頭髮總是翹起來。

- The robbers **stuck up** the bank and stole all the money.

  搶匪持槍搶劫銀行，並且拿走了所有的現金。

stick up 持槍行搶

The New Coworker

新同事

Amy tells Carl about a new coworker.
艾咪把新同事的事情告訴卡爾。

Amy: The new employee we hired is really **living up to**[1] my expectations.

Carl: Is that so? I'm glad to hear it, but I thought you didn't want to hire anyone new at your company.

Amy: Well, this one guy does the work of four people; so, in a way, hiring him has helped us **cut corners**[2].

Carl: You think he'll help **bring about**[3] some positive change, too?

Amy: Definitely. His former boss really **built up**[4] his reputation when we spoke on the phone, and I can see that he deserves it.

Carl: How so?

Amy: For example, when he starts a project, he **sticks to**[5] it until he is totally done. He also knows how to **stand up for**[6] his ideas, even if the boss disagrees.

Carl: Wow! He sounds like the perfect coworker.

艾咪： 新來的員工真的很**符合**我的期望。

卡爾： 真的嗎？真替你高興，但我以為你們公司不想聘新人。

艾咪： 嗯，這個人做了四人份的工作，所以就一定的程度來說，雇用他能幫公司**節省**成本。

卡爾： 你認為他還會**帶來**一些正面的改變嗎？

艾咪： 當然，我和他之前的老闆通過電話，他可是對他讚譽**有加**，我看得出來他說的沒錯。

卡爾： 怎麼說？

艾咪： 舉例來說，當他開始進行一項企劃後，便會**堅持**到完成。就算與老闆意見不合，他也知道要如何**支持**自己的想法。

卡爾： 哇！聽起來他是一位很理想的工作伙伴。

stick to 堅持

stand up for 維護權利；支持

1 live up to 實踐；達成

- Linda's parents were both world-famous surgeons, so she had a hard time **living up to** their expectations.
由於琳達的雙親是世界有名的外科醫生，所以她很努力地想要達成父母的期望。

- The concert was brilliant—it **lived up to** our expectations. 演唱會真是太棒了，完全符合我們的期望。

2 cut corners 節約；偷工減料

- The trick to saving money is knowing when to **cut corners**.
存錢的竅門就是要知道何時該節省開銷。

- If we **cut corners** this year, maybe we can afford to go on vacation next summer.
如果我們今年省一點，也許明年夏天就有足夠的錢能夠去度假。

3 bring about 引起；造成

- Mike **brought about** his company's collapse with his reckless spending.
麥可無盡的揮霍是造成公司倒閉的原因。

- Eleanor is the kind of woman who can **bring about** results; that's why my company hired her.
伊莉諾是個能帶來成效的女人，這就是我們公司雇用她的原因。

4 build up 增加；增強；加深印象

- Aaron is a great visionary; he **built up** a new business from nothing.
亞倫是個極有遠見的人，他白手起家，開創了新的事業。

- Natalie **built** her Spanish vocabulary **up** in preparation for her trip to Mexico.
娜塔莉學了許多西班牙文單字，為墨西哥之旅作準備。

5 stick to 堅持（通常指困境）；遵守

- I understand that you're having a hard time in this class, but just **stick to** the schedule and do the best you can.
  我知道這堂課你上得很辛苦，但你只要堅持下去、全力以赴就行了。

- It is hard to understand the class because the teacher never **sticks to** his point—he always changes the topic and never finishes any ideas.
  這門課很難理解，因為老師立場不明。他總是任意變換主題，從不下結論。

- It won't be easy to **stick to** my academic schedule because I have classes every morning at 8:30.
  我每天早上 8 點 30 分都有課，所以要我遵守課表很難。

6 stand up for 維護權利；支持

- Martin Luther King, Jr., **stood up for** the rights of his fellow African Americans.
  馬丁路德金恩捍衛了非裔美國人的權利。

- I **stood up for** my math teacher when all my friends were complaining about him.
  當我所有的朋友都在抱怨數學老師時，我卻為他挺身而出。

7 make out 填寫

- Elaine **made out** a legal will that leaves everything to her daughter.
  伊蓮在遺囑上註明會將所有財產留給她女兒。

- Jared **made** a check **out** for $50 to cover the expenses.
  傑瑞德開了一張 50 元的支票把費用付清。

8 come about 發生

- How did this terrible situation **come about**?
  怎麼會發生這麼嚴重的事情？

- Do you know how the tradition of decorating a Christmas tree **came about**?
  你知道裝飾聖誕樹的傳統是如何出現的嗎？

- How did the problem **come about** in the first place?
  問題是怎麼發生的呢？

9 die down 變少；減弱

- As the party was ending, the noise level began to **die down**.
  喧鬧聲在派對結束後逐漸消失。

- Pam's anger over her son's decision to leave school took a few weeks to **die down**.
  潘很生氣兒子決定休學，她花了好幾個星期才逐漸氣消。

- By morning, the storm had **died down**.
  暴風雨在早晨的時候逐漸平息下來。

- It was several minutes before the applause **died down**.
  掌聲持續了好幾分鐘才安靜下來。

The storm had **died down**. 暴風雨逐漸平息。

10　die out　滅絕；逐漸消失

- No one knows for sure why the dinosaurs **died out**.
  沒人知道恐龍為何會滅絕。

- The traditional customs of the native people **died out** after a few years.
  幾年後，原住民的傳統習俗漸漸消失。

- It's a custom that is beginning to **die out**.
  這項習俗正在慢慢消失。

Dinosaurs **died out** 65 million years ago.
恐龍於 6500 萬年前滅絕。

11　fade away　（影像、想法）慢慢消失；死亡

- As the harbor filled with fog, the boats **faded away**.
  船隻因為濃霧籠罩著港口而漸漸消失。

- As time went by, my childhood memories began to **fade away**.
  我的童年記憶隨著時間過去而逐漸消失。

- As the years passed, the memories **faded away**.
  記憶隨著時間的過去而逐漸消失。

fade away 慢慢消失

Falling Behind in Class
課業落後

Ricardo is telling Pauline about some troubles at school.
里卡多把在學校遇到的困難告訴寶琳。

Ricardo: Sometimes I think Ms. Conway really **has it in for**[1] me.

Pauline: Why do you say that?

Ricardo: For one thing, she seems mad at me for **falling behind**[2] in class.

Pauline: I didn't know you were behind. I guess your plans to catch up last weekend **fell through**[3].

Ricardo: Unfortunately, they did. And now both my parents and Ms. Conway want to **have it out with**[4] me.

Pauline: Did you at least prepare for tomorrow's test? Ms. Conway **gave out**[5] a handout to help us review.

Ricardo: Actually, I'm going to **hold off**[6] on studying; I'm spending all my free time trying to beat this new video game I got.

Pauline: Well, if you ask me, you should either forget about the game or **give in**[7] and accept an "F" in the class . . .

Ricardo: No way! I can pass this test without studying.

Pauline: Really? I doubt it. It seems like you **took on**[8] more classes than you can handle.

里卡多： 有時候我覺得康威女士常常**和**我**過不去**。

寶琳： 怎麼説？

里卡多： 首先，我**跟不上**學習進度，她似乎很生氣。

寶琳： 我都不曉得你跟不上進度。我想你上週末準備趕進度的計畫**泡湯了**。

里卡多： 是不幸取消了，而現在我父母和康威女士都想要**找**我**算帳**。

寶琳： 至少你會準備明天的考試吧？康威女士**發**了一張幫助我們複習的講義。

里卡多： 事實上，我的讀書計畫要**延後**了。我現在一有空，就在玩新買的電動玩具。

寶琳： 唔，我認為你應該忘掉電動，或是**默默接受**得到「F」的事實……

里卡多： 不可能！我不用唸書就可以考及格了。

寶琳： 是嗎？我很懷疑。看來你根本就無法**應付**這些課業。

080

1 have it in for 與……過不去；對……伺機報復

- Sometimes I think my tutor really **has it in for** me; no matter how hard I work, she always complains.
  有時我覺得助教常常和我過不去。無論我多用功，她老是有話要說。

- My boss must really **have it in for** me; that was the third lecture this week!
  我的老闆一定是在和我過不去，那已經是這星期第三次訓話了！

2 fall behind 落後；跟不上；延遲

- After three weeks' vacationing in the United Kingdom, Nick realized he was **falling behind** on his research project.
  尼克在英國度了三個禮拜的假後，才發現他的研究報告進度落後了。

- Frank **fell behind** on his schoolwork and couldn't graduate with his friends.
  法蘭克跟不上課業，所以無法和同學一起畢業。

- You're **falling behind** with the rent. 你遲交房租了。

3 fall through 無法實現

- Corey's plan to buy a car **fell through** when he lost his job.
  柯瑞買車的計畫在工作丟了後便告吹了。

- Wade's plan to be the coolest kid in school **fell through** when he got an embarrassing haircut.
  偉德的頭髮剪壞了，他無法成為全校最酷的小孩了。

- We found a buyer for our house, but then the sale **fell through**.
  我們找到了房子的買主，但這場交易後來告吹了。

4 have it out with 與某人起爭執

- I really **had it out with** Archie when I found out he was the one who stole my bike.

  當我發現就是阿奇偷了我的腳踏車後，便和他起了口角。

- Taylor and Lydia disagree about how best to do the project; I think they'll **have it out with** each other soon.

  泰勒和莉蒂雅對執行這項企劃的最佳方式意見不一，我認為他們很快就會吵起來。

- Judy was late for work every morning this week, and I thought I'd better **have it out with** her.

  裘蒂這星期每天早上上班都遲到，我認為我最好和她說清楚。

5 give out 分發；用盡

- To promote its new flavor of gum, the company hired some people to **give out** samples to passersby.

  公司為了宣傳新口味的口香糖，請了一些人把試吃包發給路人。

- The teacher **gave** a study guide **out** to everyone who asked for one.

  老師把學習導引手冊發給需要的人。

give out 分發

081

6 hold off 延緩發生；拖延

- They **held off** buying a new digital camera until the price went down.
  他們一直拖到數位相機降價才買了一台新的。

- I think we should **hold off** going downtown until we find the bus schedule. 找出公車時間表前，我們應該暫緩去市中心的計畫。

- **Hold off** on calling a taxi; maybe my aunt can give us a ride.
  先別叫計程車，也許我阿姨可以載我們一程。

7 give in 讓步；投降

- I know you're not the best football player, but you shouldn't **give in** and quit the team without trying a little harder.
  我知道你並非最棒的足球員，但你不應該沒再多試幾個星期，就輕易放棄和退出球隊。

- After a few months of trying to live without a TV, I finally **gave in** and bought one.
  過了幾個月沒有電視的日子後，我終於放棄且買了一台新的。

- I finally **gave in** and let him stay up to watch TV.
  我終於讓步，讓他熬夜看電視。

8 take on 承擔；聘僱

- I'm not sure if I can **take on** any more classes; my schedule is already full.
  我不確定我是否能應付多修幾門課，我的課表很滿了。

- My company **took on** three new employees last week.
  我們公司上星期聘用了三位新員工。

9   take down 取下；寫下

- After Florence's art exhibit, the workers **took down** all of the paintings that hadn't sold.
  佛羅倫斯的展覽結束後，工作人員把所有沒賣出的畫拿了下來。

- Jim's mom made him **take** the rock 'n' roll posters **down** from his wall.
  吉姆的媽媽要他把牆上的搖滾樂團海報拿下來。

- Did you **take down** any notes during physics class?
  你有抄物理課的筆記嗎？

take down 取下

10   hold out 堅持；給予

- Don't buy the first car you find; **hold out** until you see the perfect model.
  別買你第一輛看到的車，要堅持到你看到最理想的車款才下手。

- The waiter **held out** a tray of drinks and offered them to everyone at the party.
  服務生把飲料放在托盤上，給所有參加派對的人喝。

Breaking Up[1]
分手 [082]

Gavin calls Judy on the phone.
蓋文打電話給裘蒂。

Gavin: Hello, Judy! It's me, Gavin.

Judy: Gavin? Please **leave** me **alone**[2]! I told you never to call me again!

Gavin: Judy, please don't **break off**[3] our relationship. I know that things have been very **touch and go**[4] between us lately, but I miss you! I must see you again.

Judy: I don't think so. Your attitude really **wears** me **down**[5]. You can drop by one more time, but only so you can **bring back**[6] those CDs I lent you.

Gavin: And that's it? After that, I must **let** you **alone**[7]?

Judy: Yes. Although we had some good times, **on the whole**[8] our romance was pretty boring. I'm sorry, but it's over!

wear down 使疲累

leave sb. alone 讓某人獨處

蓋文： 哈囉，裘蒂！我是蓋文。

裘蒂： 蓋文？請不要**煩**我！我說過別再打電話給我！

蓋文： 裘蒂，拜託不要**結束**我們的關係。我知道最近我們的關係變得**岌岌可危**，但我很想念妳！我一定要見妳。

裘蒂： 我覺得不需要。你的態度真的令我很**累**。唔，我們再見一面吧，只有這樣你才可以把我借給你的 CD **還**給我。

蓋文： 就這樣？之後我便**不再打擾**你？

裘蒂： 是的。雖然我們在一起很快樂，但這段感情**大致來說**非常無趣。很抱歉，我們之間結束了！

1 break up 打碎；分手

- I've just **broken up** with my boyfriend.
  我才剛和男朋友分手。

- The company has been **broken up** and sold off.
  這家公司已經解散，並且廉價售出了。

2 leave (sb or sth) alone 讓某人獨處；別打擾

- **Leave** Rick **alone**. He's making a very important phone call. 別打擾瑞克，他在講一通很重要的電話。

- When you clean up my yard, please **leave** that tree **alone**. Don't cut it down or trim its branches; I like it the way it is.
  打掃院子時，請不要管那棵樹。別砍掉，也別修剪葉子，我喜歡現在這樣。

3 break off 分離；中斷

- Corey **broke off** a piece of the cookie and gave it to his younger brother.
  柯瑞把餅乾分成一小塊給弟弟。

- Can you **break** me **off** a piece of that chocolate?
  可以分一塊巧克力給我嗎？

- When the phone rang, Mrs. Williams **broke off** the conversation and ran to answer it.
  電話聲響起時，威廉斯太太停止了談話，然後跑向電話。

4 touch and go 情況危急；不到最後無法定論

- The dental work was going well at first, but then it was **touch and go** for a while.
  牙醫的工作剛開始很正常，但後來有一段時間不是很順利。

- Marc wasn't sure if he had passed his exams; it was really **touch and go**.
  馬克不確定他考試是否及格，不到最後關頭真的無法論定。

5   wear down 使疲累

- This boring class really **wears** me **down**; I'm always nearly asleep before it's even half over!
  這堂無聊的課把我累壞了，通常課還不到一半我就快要睡著！

- The long job interview **wore** Harriet **down** because it was so difficult and tiring.
  這個既難熬又累人的漫長工作面試把哈莉特給累壞了。

6   bring back 歸還；憶起

- If you go to the store, can you **bring back** some ice cream?
  如果你要去商店，可以帶些冰淇淋回來嗎？

7   let (sb) alone 不打擾某人做某事（※少用）

- **Let** Seth **alone**. He's trying to finish his report.
  別煩塞斯，他正試著要完成報告。

- I wish she would **let** me **alone** so I could get some sleep.
  我希望她不要來打擾我，這樣我才可以睡點覺。

8   on the whole 概括；就整體而言

- **On the whole**, my vacation was excellent, though there were a few problems.
  即便我放假時遇到了一些困難，我的假期整體而言還是很棒。

- It was a fun party **on the whole**, but I wish the music had been better.
  整體而言，這個派對很好玩，但我希望音樂能有所改善。

- **On the whole**, I think my dinner party was a success.
  整體而言，我認為這次的晚餐聚會辦得很成功。

- We have had some bad times, but **on the whole** we're fairly happy.
  我們遇到了一些不開心的事情，但整體來說我們還是過得很快樂。

9 lay off 停止；節制；解僱

- My coworkers didn't **lay off** our boss for the entire dinner; they were very critical of her.
  用餐時，我的同事毫不客氣地批評老闆，他們對她非常不滿。

- I usually run several miles every day but **lay off** in the hot weather.
  我每天通常會跑好幾英里，
  但在大熱天就不跑了。

- He was **laid off** along with many others when the company moved to New York City.
  公司搬遷至紐約市時，
  他和許多員工都被解僱了。

be laid off 被解僱

10 wear off 逐漸消失

- As soon as the coffee began to **wear off**, Jill felt tired.
  隨著咖啡的效用逐漸消失，吉爾感覺很累。

- When the aspirin **wore off**, Lou's headache returned.
  當阿斯匹靈逐漸失去效用時，盧的頭又痛了起來。

- The effect of the injection will gradually **wear off**.
  打針後的藥效會逐漸消失。

11 let up 停止；減弱；天氣轉晴

- If the snow ever **lets up**, we'll drive to the store.
  如果停止下雪，我們就會開車去商店。

- When the rain **lets up,** we'll go for a walk.
  我們雨停後就去散步。

- The rain shows no sign of **letting up**.
  雨一點也沒有要停的樣子。

12 wait up for 為了等某人而不睡覺；停下來等某人

- Mom was **waiting up for** me when I walked in the door, and she was not happy!
  當我回到家時發現媽媽還在等我，而且她不太高興！

- If you're planning on returning home before midnight, I'll try to **wait up for** you.
  如果你打算在午夜前回家，我會等你的。

- We're so far ahead of our friends; let's **wait up for** them here.
  我們超前了朋友許多，我們在這裡等他們吧。

- I'll probably be out very late tonight, so don't **wait up for** me.
  我今天晚上會很晚才回來，所以不要為我等門了。

- Let's **wait up for** Sherry to see how her date went.
  我們等雪莉回來吧，了解一下她的約會是否進展順利。

Being a Designer
成為設計師 🎧 085

Amanda has some excellent news to share with Joy.
亞曼達有天大的好消息要和喬伊分享。

Amanda: I've got great news! You know that I **have my heart set on**[1] becoming a designer and have worked a lot lately on making my own clothes.

Joy: So what's the news? Did your style **catch on**[2]?

Amanda: It sure did! It seems I'm really **cut out for**[3] fashion design.

Joy: Why? What happened, exactly?

Amanda: Well, I was showing a few samples to a local store, and they loved the style so much that they **bought up**[4] everything. The next day, they called to tell me that everything had already **sold out**[5].

Joy: Fantastic! Did you make a lot of money?

Amanda: Yup! It **works out**[6] to about a 200% profit for me.

Joy: Congratulations!

亞曼達： 好消息！因為我**已經下定決心**要成為一名設計師，所以我最近都在設計衣服。

喬伊： 所以妳要告訴我的消息是什麼？是妳設計的衣服**廣受歡迎**嗎？

亞曼達： 沒錯！看來我真的很**適合**成為一位服裝設計師。

喬伊： 怎麼說？究竟怎麼回事？

亞曼達： 嗯，我拿了一些樣本到這附近的一家店，他們非常喜歡我的設計，而且全數**買下**。隔天，他們還打電話跟我說衣服全**賣完**了。

喬伊： 真了不起！妳賺了不少吧？

亞曼達： 是啊！我**一共**約賺了兩倍的利潤。

喬伊： 恭喜妳！

buy up 全部買下

sell out 銷售一空

171

1 have one's heart set on 下定決心；一心想要

- I **had my heart set on** becoming a doctor.
  我已經下定決心要成為一名醫生了。

- Sarah **has her heart set on** going to Bermuda next year.
  莎拉下定決心明年要去百慕達。

2 catch on 受到歡迎；聽懂（意思或玩笑）

- The new clothing brand has really **caught on** among college students.
  這個新牌子的衣服很受到大學生的歡迎。

- Raul didn't **catch on** that we were making fun of him.
  勞爾聽不懂我們在開他玩笑。

3 be cut out for 勝任；適合

- Darren **is** not **cut out for** a job in a big company.
  戴倫不適合在大公司工作。

- Francesca **is cut out for** environmental work with her master's degree in natural science.
  法蘭契斯卡擁有自然科學碩士學位，她很適合環保工作。

4 buy up 全部買下

- Tabitha **bought** all the chocolate **up** because she was crazy for it.
  由於泰貝莎超愛吃巧克力，所以她買下了所有的巧克力。

- Flynn **bought up** all the batteries in the store because he needed them for his stereo.
  佛林為了音響而買下了這家店所有的電池。

- Chris **bought up** all the land in the surrounding area.
  克里斯買下了附近所有的土地。

5 sell out 銷售一空；出清

- The new edition of his book **sold out** in just a few hours!
  他的書出了新版本，幾個小時內便銷售一空了！

- The store **sells out** of ice cream whenever it is hot.
  每當天氣很熱時，店裡的冰淇淋便會銷售一空。

6 work out 總共；健身；擬定（計畫）；解決；想出；得到……的結果

- The total cost **worked out** to around $400.
  一共約 400 元。

- Emmy wants to be healthier, so she **works out** three times a week.
  艾咪想要健康的身體，所以每星期會做三次運動。

- Byron **worked out** a way to save a lot of money over the summer.
  拜倫想出了一個夏天的省錢大計。

7 back out 反悔；食言；退出

- Although Bryan had agreed to buy Tracy an espresso machine, he **backed out** and gave her a new purse instead.
  雖然布萊恩答應買一台咖啡機給崔西，但他改變主意買了一個新皮包給她。

- Laura **backed out** of her work contract and quit.
  蘿拉中止工作合約後便辭職了。

8 back up 聲援；倒車

- The central idea of your research paper is very interesting, but you need to **back** it **up** with some evidence.

  你的研究報告的論點非常吸引人，不過你需要一些證據來支持這個論點。

- A good theory is **backed up** with observations and data.

  完整的學說會以觀測資料作為支援。

- The taxi driver passed by my apartment, so he had to **back up**.

  計程車司機駛過了我家公寓，所以他必須倒車。

back up 倒車

9 throw out 丟棄；驅逐；駁回（意見、計畫等）；提出

- Those shoes are really old; it's time to **throw** them **out**.

  這些鞋子真的很舊了；該丟了。

- Tim got **thrown out** of the club because he tried to start a fight with some people.

  提姆因為險些釀成打群架而被趕出俱樂部。

- Let me **throw** this concept **out** to you and see if you like it.

  請讓我提出我的想法，再看看你是否喜歡。

- The lawsuit was **thrown out** of court because there wasn't enough evidence.

  這件訴訟案因證據不足而被法院駁回了。

10 throw up 嘔吐;產生新想法或問題;提起

- Diane had a stomachache and **threw up** on the school bus.

  黛安胃痛,於是在校車上吐了。

- The discussion group **threw up** some great ideas.

  這個討論小組想出了一些很棒的方法。(英式用法)

11 clear up 清理;釐清;天氣轉晴

- Joanne's doctor **cleared up** any questions about her worsening health.

  瓊安的醫生釐清了她健康每況愈下的因素。

- Wade asked his tutor to help **clear up** his confusion about the English homework.

  偉德請家庭老師幫忙釐清他做英文作業時遇到的難題。

- The sky began to **clear up** in the afternoon, so football practice wasn't canceled after all.

  下午天空開始放晴,所以足球練習並沒有取消。

clear up 天氣轉晴

The Ruined Cake
毀掉的蛋糕

Suzie and Emory are chatting about a ruined cake.
蘇西和艾墨利在聊一個毀掉的蛋糕。

Suzie: I'm so upset! The cake I made last night is ruined! Oh boy, I worked so hard on it . . .

Emory: Don't **beat around the bush**[1]! Just tell me what happened.

Suzie: Someone left it uncovered in the fridge, and it **dried out**[2]. It looks like someone took a bite out of it as well! It looks terrible.

Emory: I bet your roommate was just **fooling around**[3]. He probably did it as a joke.

Suzie: No, I think he did it to **get even with**[4] me. He's trying to **stir up**[5] a fight!

Emory: **Slow down**[6]! you're talking too fast. Do you really think he **is up to something**[7]?

Suzie: There's no question. He's still mad at me for **putting an end to**[8] his dream of becoming a famous architect by accidentally spilling coffee all over his designs.

Emory: Aha! Well, that explains things . . .

蘇西： 我好生氣！我昨晚做的蛋糕全毀了！天啊，我可是費盡心力耶……

艾墨利： **講話別兜圈子**了！快告訴我怎麼回事。

蘇西： 有人沒把蛋糕蓋上盒蓋就放入冰箱，整個蛋糕都**乾掉**了，好像還有人偷吃了一口！真糟糕。

艾墨利： 我賭是妳室友**搞的鬼**。他可能只是開個玩笑。

蘇西： 不，我認為他是在**報復**我。他只是想要**激怒**我，和我吵一架！

艾墨利： 說**慢一點**，妳講太快了。妳真的認為他在**盤算**些什麼嗎？

蘇西： 沒錯。他還在氣我不小心把咖啡灑在他的設計圖上，害他**結束**了成為名建築師的夢想。

艾墨利： 啊哈！唔，這不就解釋了一切……

1 **beat around the bush** 說話拐彎抹角

- Kyle was embarrassed to tell his boss that he was quitting, so he **beat around the bush** for a while.
  凱爾不好意思告訴老闆他要辭職，所以他講話一直兜圈子。

- Lyle **beat around the bush** before he asked Jenna to the prom.
  萊爾在邀請珍娜參加舞會前，講話一直拐彎抹角。

- Quit **beating around the bush** and tell me what you really think about my idea.
  別拐彎抹角了，告訴我你覺得我的意見如何。

- Don't **beat around the bush**—get to the point!
  別拐彎抹角了，有話就直說吧！

2 **dry out** 使變乾

- The potatoes I left in the sun **dried out** and became hard.
  我放在太陽底下曬乾的馬鈴薯變硬了。

- In the countryside, people sometimes hang meat in the sun so it **dries out**.
  在鄉下，人們有時會把肉掛在太陽底下曬乾。

3 **fool around** 開玩笑；遊手好閒

- Ed **fooled around** all weekend and didn't do any work.
  艾迪週末都在鬼混沒寫作業。

- Don't **fool around** in class, or the teacher will call your parents!
  上課別打混，否則老師會打電話給你的父母！

- Jimmy is always getting in trouble for **fooling around** in class.
  吉米老是因為上課打混而惹上麻煩。

4   get even with 報復

- Jackie decided to **get even with** Mohammed for teasing her in front of her friends.
  穆罕默德在賈姬朋友的面前取笑她，所以賈姬決定報復他。

- How do you plan to **get even with** Juliana for ruining your party?
  茱莉安娜破壞了你的派對，你打算如何報復她？

- I want to **get even with** the guy who hit me with the ball.
  我想報復用球打我的人。

5   stir up   激起；引起問題

- Looking at her high school yearbook **stirred up** some sad memories for poor Tina.
  可憐的緹娜在看高中畢業紀念冊時，激起了許多不愉快的回憶。

- The fight between the two boys **stirred** the problem **up** even more.
  這兩個男孩之間的爭吵引起了更嚴重的紛爭。

6   slow down 放慢速度；放輕鬆

- You're driving close to a school; please **slow down**.
  你開到學校附近了，請開慢一點。

- I wish the driver would **slow** the bus **down**;
  he's driving dangerously fast!
  我希望有人能讓公車司機開慢一點，開這麼快很危險！

- The doctor told him to **slow down** or he'll have a heart attack.
  醫生要他放輕鬆，否則會得心臟病。

7 be up to something 策劃;盤算

- Eli is acting pretty strange; I think he **is up to something**.
  依萊最近舉止怪異,我想他在暗中盤算些什麼。

- It seems as if Carl **is up to something**—he's probably planning a surprise party.
  卡爾看來在策劃些什麼,他可能打算辦一場驚喜派對。

8 put an end to 終結

- The ringing phone **put an end to** our private conversation.
  我們的談話因為電話聲響起而結束。

- A terrible rainstorm **put an end to** our day at the beach.
  一場暴風雨來襲,結束了我們在海邊的行程。

9 come to an end 終結

- There is an English idiom that says "All good things must **come to an end**."
  「天下無不散的筵席」是一句英文諺語。

- When my boss asked for our opinions, I thought the meeting would never **come to an end**.
  當老闆問起我們的意見,我感覺這個會議永遠不會結束。

10 look out on 面對

- Sam's new apartment **looks out on** the Brooklyn Bridge.
  山姆的新公寓正對著布魯克林大橋。

- The five-star hotel **looks out on** the ocean.
  這間五星級飯店面對著大海。

11 take in

學習；理解；欺騙；
拜訪；（衣服）改小

- Gwen was very interested in the class, so she **took in** everything the professor said.

  關對這門課非常有興趣，所以她把所有教授說的話都記住了。

- The old lady was **taken in** by the used car salesman, who convinced her to buy a car she didn't want.

  這位老太太被賣二手車的推銷員騙了，他說服她買了一台她不想要的車。

- During their first night in Paris, the happy couple walked around and **took in** the sights.

  在抵達巴黎的第一個夜晚，這對幸福的夫妻四處拜訪了許多名勝。

- I'll have to **take** this dress **in** at the waist. It's too big.

  我必須把這件洋裝的腰圍改小，它太大了。

take in （衣服）改小

Moving Away From Home
離家 🎧 [091]

Emma asks Marcus what his family thinks of his plan to move to Nebraska.
艾瑪詢問馬克斯關於他的家人對他計畫搬到內布拉斯加州的看法。

Emma: How did your dad take the news that you've decided to move to Nebraska?

Marcus: Actually, he really **kept his head**[1]. At first, he thought I was **putting** him **on**[2].

Emma: And when he found out you were serious?

Marcus: Well, **it goes without saying**[3] that he'd prefer me to stay at home, but I guess he isn't as narrow-minded as I thought.

Emma: And how about your mom? Did she **lose her head**[4]?

Marcus: Yeah, my mom's different. As soon as I began to tell her the news, she **cut** me **short**[5] and told me I was **wasting my breath**[6].

Emma: Boy! You must really be **on edge**[7] now!

艾瑪：　　你爸對於你要搬到內布拉斯加州的看法如何？

馬克斯：　事實上，他還挺**冷靜**的。他起初以為我在**騙**他。

艾瑪：　　那他發現你是認真後的反應是？

馬克斯：　唔，**那還用說**，他當然希望我待在家裡，但他不像我想像中的不開明。

艾瑪：　　那你媽覺得如何呢？她有**慌了手腳**嗎？

馬克斯：　是啊，我媽的反應就不同了。我才一提起這件事情，她便**打斷**了我的話，還說我在**白費唇舌**。

艾瑪：　　天啊，那你現在一定**坐立難安**！

keep one's head 保持冷靜

lose one's head 失去理智

183

092

1 keep one's head 保持冷靜；沉著

- One of Juliet's best qualities is her ability to **keep her head** when things seem totally crazy.
即便事情失控，茱麗葉也能夠保持冷靜，這就是她的個人特質之一。
- Calm down and **keep your head**; there's no reason to get stressed out. 保持鎮定，沒必要那麼緊張。

2 put (sb) on（以開玩笑的方式）欺騙他人

- You told me that you were going to study, and now I see you at the movies; it looks like you were **putting me on**. 你說要去唸書，但我現在發現你在看電影，看來你是在騙我。
- I didn't really win a sailboat; I was just **putting you on**.
我並沒有贏得一艘帆船，我只是騙你的。

3 (it) goes without saying 不用說

- **It goes without saying** that in today's world, time is money.
在現今的社會，不用說，時間就是金錢。
- **It goes without saying** that if you want to go to Harvard, you'd better get good grades.
如果你想進入哈佛，不用說成績要很好。

4 lose one's head 失去理智

- I was so frightened that I **lost my head** completely.
我很害怕到完全失去理智了。
- Although Tim is usually calm in class, for some reason he really **lost his head** today.
提姆上課通常都很安靜，但他今天為了一些因素而失控了。
- Erin **lost her head** in the meeting this afternoon, and our boss fired her. 艾琳今天下午開會時情緒失控，所以老闆把她解僱了。
- I usually stay quite calm in meetings, but this time I just **lost my head**. 我開會時通常都很冷靜，但這次我真的失去理智了。

5 cut short 打斷談話；中斷

- While Wanda was telling Chris a boring story about her day at work, he **cut** her **short** and turned on the TV.
  當汪達在告訴克里斯辦公室發生的無趣瑣事時，他打斷了她，並把電視打開。

- James **cut** his workday **short** to go home early.
  詹姆斯結束工作，提早回家。

- Just as Alfredo was getting to the funny part of the joke, his cell phone rang and **cut** him **short**.
  當阿爾弗雷多正要進入笑話最精采的部分時，手機鈴聲打斷了他。

- I started to explain, but she **cut** me **short**, saying she had to catch a bus.
  我開始解釋時，她打斷了我的話，說她必須去趕公車了。

6 waste one's breath 白費唇舌

- Don't **waste your breath**—I've already asked him to help, and he said no.
  別白費唇舌了，我已經請他幫忙了，但他不願意。

- Phillip is so stubborn; don't **waste your breath** making suggestions.
  菲力普很固執，別浪費唇舌提供他意見。

- Eddy lectured his sister on how dangerous it is to go out alone in the city at night. However, he was just **wasting his breath** because she wasn't listening.
  艾迪告訴妹妹晚上獨自到市區很危險，但他只是在白費唇舌而已，她根本沒在聽。

- Honestly, you're **wasting your breath**—she doesn't want to hear what anyone else has to say.
  老實說你在白費唇舌，她並不想要聽其他人的看法。

093

7   on edge   緊張；提心吊膽

- My sisters and I were **on edge** while we waited to hear whether our flight was delayed.
  在等待飛機是否會延誤的消息時，我姊妹和我很緊張。

- It was the night before her first day of college, and Mel was **on edge**.
  梅兒上大學的前一個晚上非常緊張。

- Is something wrong? You seem a bit **on edge** this morning.
  怎麼了嗎？你今天早上看起來有點不安。

- You're always **on edge** waiting for an important call because you don't know when the phone will ring.
  你在等重要電話的時候總是很不安，因為你無法得知電話何時會響。

8   get the better of   打敗；戰勝

- Although my teammates and I played our best, the other team **got the better of** us.
  雖然我們球隊打得很好，但我們還是被別支球隊打敗了。

- My brother **got the better of** his asthma and rarely gets sick anymore.
  自從我哥哥的氣喘病治癒了後，他便很少生病了。

- Her curiosity **got the better of** her, and she opened the letter.
  她在好奇心的驅使下，打開了信。

9 **go through** 找出；經歷；大量使用

- Olivia is **going through** her closet to find some clothes to donate to charity.
  奧立薇亞翻遍了衣櫃，找出一些衣服捐給慈善機構。

- We'd better let Seth relax; he **went through** a terrible situation at school today.
  我們最好讓塞斯休息一下，他今天在學校經歷了很不愉快的事情。

- My Italian friend **goes through** so much pasta because she eats it for lunch and dinner every day.
  我的義大利朋友吃了很多義大利麵，她每天中餐和晚餐都會吃。

10 **break loose** 掙脫；逃跑

- We saw a movie where the hero is tied to a chair but he manages to **break loose**.
  我們看了一部電影，劇中的男主角被綁在椅子上，但他後來設法掙脫了。

- During the thunderstorm, all three horses **broke loose** from the barn and ran into the forest because they were scared.
  暴風雨來襲時，這三匹馬因害怕而從馬廄逃了出來，跑進了森林裡面。

11 **stand up** 讓人白等；證實

- The information Joel used in his report will never **stand up** to critical review.
  喬爾報告中的資料無法證實這篇評論。

- I had planned to take Martin out for dinner, but he **stood** me **up** and never showed up.
  我原本打算帶馬汀出去吃晚餐，但他放我鴿子，沒有出現。

- Their evidence will never **stand up** in court.
  他們的證據在法庭上永遠無法證實。

Being Kicked Out of School 被退學

32

Amy tells Arthur about getting kicked out of the university.
愛咪告訴亞瑟有關她被退學的事情。

Arthur:	What did your mom say when you told her that you were kicked out of the university?
Amy:	She really **went off the deep end**[1].
Arthur:	Well, I suppose that's understandable. After all, you did copy some texts in your report; you really did **goof up**[2].
Amy:	But it's not fair! I didn't know doing this would be such a big problem! I never knew that copying texts would **screw up**[3] my life so much. And nothing I do helps. I've been **kissing up to**[4] the teacher of that class, but she doesn't care.
Arthur:	Kissing up isn't the best way to deal with this problem. You've really **lost your touch**[5], Amy. You used to be a model student, **more or less**[6]. Now you have to **step down**[7] from your position on the debate team and from your role in the honor society.
Amy:	What a disaster!

亞瑟： 妳媽知道你被學校退學後有說什麼嗎？

愛咪： 她**大發雷霆**。

亞瑟： 嗯，我想那是可以理解的。畢竟，你真的抄襲了別人的文章。你真的是**大錯特錯**。

愛咪： 可是太不公平了！我不知這樣做會引起這麼大的麻煩！我又不曉得抄襲他人的文章會**搞砸**我的人生。我後來想要補救，但是都沒有用。我一直想去**討好**該科老師，但她都不理我。

亞瑟： 討好老師不是處理這個問題的最佳方式。愛咪，你真是太**沒有經驗**了。**好歹**你以前也是模範生。現在你得**退出**辯論社和榮譽學會了。

愛咪： 真是糟透了！

go off the deep end 大發雷霆　　screw up 搞砸

095

1 **go off the deep end** 勃然大怒

- Alan was a great guy until he **went off the deep end** and started gambling all the time.
  艾倫在脾氣變差、開始賭博前，一直是個好好先生。

- When Daphne told her father that she had crashed his car, he was so mad that he **went off the deep end**.
  當達芙妮告訴父親她把他的車撞壞時，他勃然大怒。

2 **goof up** 犯錯

- Valerie **goofed up** and showed up at the university on Saturday.
  薇樂麗搞錯日子了，她星期六還跑去學校。

- If I go near a skateboard, I'm sure I will **goof up** and fall off.
  我若是站在滑板上，肯定會玩不好摔下來。

3 **screw up** 搞砸；使混淆；傷害

- The waiter **screwed** Mira's order **up** and brought her mashed potatoes instead of French fries.
  服務生弄錯了米拉的餐點，他應該要送薯條過來，而不是馬鈴薯泥。

- Nicole really **screwed** Sam **up** when she left him.
  妮可離開山姆時真的把他傷得很重。

4 **kiss up to** (someone) 討好

- Amanda always **kisses up to** her boss when she wants to take a day off.
  每當亞曼達想休假時，她都會討好老闆。

- Kyle **kisses up to** our soccer coach because he thinks it will help him get promoted to team captain.
  凱爾老是在討好足球隊教練，因為他認為這樣做就能成為隊長。

5   lose one's touch 變生疏

- Although Gene's first book was a bestseller, it seems he **lost his touch**—his second book is not so good.
  雖然金的第一本書非常暢銷，但他顯然退步不少。他的第二本書就沒賣那麼好了。

- When I watched my favorite actress in her newest movie, I saw that she still hasn't **lost her touch**.
  我最愛的演員在最新的電影中，演技可是一點都沒退步。

- The goalkeeper's performance in the game shows he is not **losing his touch**.
  守門員在這場競賽的表現一點也沒有變生疏。

6   more or less 差不多；大約

- Going on vacation was **more or less** worthwhile; the only problem was that it rained the entire time.
  這假期大致上來說都很好，唯一的問題是一直在下雨。

- This bag weighs 20 pounds, **more or less**.
  這袋東西大約重 20 磅。

- The project was **more or less** a success.
  這項企劃大致上來說是成功的。

7   step down 下來；退休；辭職；減少

- Biff **stepped down** from the ladder and shook Hank's hand.
  比夫從梯子上下來與漢克握手。

- We need to hire a new manager at our company because the last one just **stepped down**.
  我們公司需要聘請一位新的經理，上任經理才剛退休。

- After Ronny got in trouble for taking too long of a vacation, his boss asked him to **step down**.
  朗尼因休假太長而造成困擾，老闆要求他自動請辭。

8   step in   介入

- When Luke saw his sisters arguing, he **stepped in** and helped them reach an agreement.
  路克介入了他兩位姊姊的爭吵之中，幫助他們達成協議。

- I know you haven't asked for my advice, but please let me **step in**.
  我知道你沒有問我的意見，但請容我插句話。

- When Isabelle couldn't teach the class, her sister **stepped in** and gave the lesson.
  伊莎貝爾無法授課，她的姊姊到學校代她上課。

- After the leading actress broke her leg, Jane **stepped in** and played the role.
  女主角摔斷了腿後，珍加入並且接下了這個角色。

9   step on (someone) 受到不平等的待遇

- Sometimes the nicest people get **stepped on** the most.
  心地善良的人有時會受到最不平等的待遇。

- You should be more confident and stop letting people **step on** you.
  你應該對自己要有點信心，別再被其他人欺負了。

10   in hand   在掌握中；在控制中；在進行中

- Regarding the matter **in hand**, I suggest we cancel the next meeting.
  就目前這件事情而論，我認為應該取消下次會議。

- Because Elaine's birthday is next week, the preparations for the party should be well **in hand** by now.
  伊蓮的生日就在下星期，派對現在應該都準備好了。

11　on hand　在手邊；在附近；待執行

- If you don't have a calculator **on hand**, please ask to use your partner's.
  如果你手邊沒有計算機，請向組員借。

- I need to make a phone call; do you have your cell phone **on hand**?
  我需要打通電話，你身上有手機嗎？

on hand 在手邊

12　a steal　買到便宜貨

- I can't believe you found a computer for only $100—what **a steal**!
  我不敢相信你買了一台才 100 塊錢的電腦，真是個意外收穫！

- I bought this used cell phone at a good price; it was **a** real **steal**!
  我用很便宜的價格買下了這支中古手機，真是賺到了！

Kicking the Habit
戒掉惡習 🎧 097

Ronald tells Wendy about his new plan.
羅納德把新計畫告訴溫蒂。

Wendy: Why are you smiling? Something must be **looking up**[1] for you.

Ronald: You got it! I'm in a good mood because I've been **kicking around**[2] an interesting idea .

Wendy: What's the idea? Tell me!

Ronald: Well, I noticed yesterday that I had gained five more pounds, and that's the **last straw**[3]. I watch too much TV, and I'm too fat. It's time for me to **kick the habit**[4] of eating junk food and being lazy.

Wendy: Sounds like you're really **on the ball**[5] with this idea. But what are you going to do?

Ronald: A group of friends and I will **put together**[6] a basketball team, and we'll practice three times a week. This way, we'll all have a good time. I can lose some weight, and when my girlfriend sees how good I look, maybe she'll want to **make up with**[7] me. So, you want to join us?

Wendy: No thanks. I'm going home to watch a movie and eat some pizza—but have fun!

溫蒂：　　　你為何笑得這麼開心呢？一定是有什麼**好**事。

羅納德：　　沒錯！我的心情很好，因為我一直在**思考**一項有趣的計畫。

溫蒂：　　　什麼計畫？快告訴我！

羅納德：　　唔，我昨天發現體重增加了五磅，我**不能再這樣下去**了。我看太多電視，吃太多東西了。我該**戒掉**吃垃圾食物和懶惰的**壞習慣**了。

溫蒂：　　　看來你已經很**清楚**你的想法了，但你要怎麼做呢？

羅納德：　　我會和一群朋友**組成**一支籃球隊，每個星期練三次球。這樣一來我們可以玩得很愉快，而我的體重也會減輕。等我女朋友看到我帥氣的模樣時，她也許會想和我**重修舊好**。所以，妳想不想加入我們呢？

溫蒂：　　　不，謝了。我想回家看電影，吃批薩，反正你開心就好！

kick around 考慮

kick the habit 戒掉壞習慣

195

1 look up 變好

- Ever since Jasmine got a raise at work, things have been **looking up**.
  賈斯敏加薪後，一切都變得很美好。

- Things are really **looking up** this semester, and I'm getting excellent grades.
  這學期一切都變得很順利，而我的成績也很優異。

- I hope things will start to **look up** in the new year.
  我希望在新的一年事情會變得很順利。

2 kick (sth) around 討論；考慮

- We **kicked around** the plan of going on vacation in Spain, but in the end we never went.
  我們一直在討論西班牙之旅的計畫，但我們最後並沒有去成。

- Agatha **kicked around** the idea of studying psychology, but in the end, she decided not to.
  雅嘉考慮過是否要修心理學這門課，但她最後還是決定放棄。

- I need to get everyone together so we can **kick** a few ideas **around**. 我必須把所有人聚集在一起，討論一些想法。

3 last straw 已達極限

- There's a well-known English proverb that says it's "the **last straw** that breaks the camel's back."
  「壓垮駱駝的最後一根稻草」是一句著名的英文諺語。

- Saul's car breaking down on the way to work was pretty bad, but when it broke down again on the way home, that was the **last straw**.
  索爾的車在上班途中壞掉已經很不幸了，然而車子又在回家路上拋錨，真是衰到了極點。

- Paula has always been rude to me, but it was the **last straw** when she started insulting my mother.
  實拉對我一直很沒有禮貌，但令人忍無可忍的是她開始羞辱我的母親。

4   kick the habit 戒掉壞習慣

- Steven used to be a heavy smoker, but he **kicked the habit** last year.
  史帝芬曾經是個老菸槍，
  但他去年戒菸了。

- Ike finally **kicked his bad habit** of biting his fingernails.
  艾克最後終於戒掉咬手指甲的壞習慣了。

- Researchers said smokers who **kick the habit** have less chance of developing cancer.
  研究人員表示，已戒菸的人罹患癌症的機率會較低。

5   be on the ball 快速理解；反應靈敏

- After his third cup of coffee, Harry **was** really **on the ball**.
  哈利在喝了三杯咖啡之後，終於清醒了。

- After getting little sleep the night before, Corey **was not on the ball**.
  柯伊昨晚沒什麼睡，所以頭腦不清楚。

6   put together 組合

- Taylor really knows a lot about motorcycles. If you give him all the parts, he can **put** one **together**!
  泰勒真的很懂摩托車。只要給他所有的零件，他就可以組裝好！

- Model airplanes come in pieces that have to be **put together**.
  模型飛機是一片片的，必須組裝起來。

7   make up with (sb) 與某人重修舊好

- After the argument, Taylor **made up with** Rachel by giving her some flowers.
  爭吵過後，泰勒送花給瑞秋，和她重修舊好。

- Joel and Alice had a big fight, and I'm not sure if they'll ever **make up with** one another.
  喬爾和艾莉絲大吵了一架，我不確定他們是否還會合好如初。

8   make up   捏造；組成；化妝；和解

- Because Ron didn't want to go to the party, he **made** an excuse **up** about having to write a report.
  因為朗不想參加派對，所以他用寫報告作為藉口。

- Kate **made up** a great story about a princess, which she told her daughter at bedtime.
  凱特在女兒睡前念了一個虛構的公主故事。

- Two halves **make up** a whole.
  把兩個二分之一合起來就變成了一整個。

- The fashion model was all **made up** for the photo shoot.
  時尚模特兒已完妝準備照片拍攝的工作。

- They kissed and **made up**, as usual.
  他們親吻對方，然後合好，一如往常。

9   cover up   掩蓋（秘密）

- Will tried to **cover up** the fact that he was caught cheating, but everyone found out about it.
  威爾企圖掩飾他考試作弊被抓的事實，但大家都發現了。

- If you are caught doing something illegal, it may not be a good idea to **cover** it **up**.
  做違法的事情如果被抓到，最好不要企圖隱瞞。

- The company tried to **cover up** its employment of illegal immigrants.
  公司企圖掩蓋雇用非法移民的事實。

- I was amazed that the building contractors we hired tried to **cover up** the problems they had.
  我很意外我們所聘用的建築承包商竟然企圖掩飾他們所遇到的問題。

10   drop off   在途中下車；減少

- Melissa **dropped off** her passport at the hotel and then went off to explore Paris.
  瑪莉莎將護照留在飯店後，便開始在巴黎觀光。

- Jordan **dropped off** her sister at the park and then went to the movies.
  喬登讓妹妹在公園下車後，便去看電影。

- The price of plane tickets to California always **drops off** after the summer.
  夏天過後，飛往加州的機票總是會降價。

- The demand for mobile phones shows no signs of **dropping off**.
  人們對於手機的需求一點也沒有減少的現象。

drop off 在途中下車

11   turn over   翻過來；移交

- In the middle of the night, Nancy **turned over** and slept on her back.
  南西在半夜翻了個身，變成仰躺。

- Before leaving her job, Dolores **turned over** her tasks to a coworker.
  辭職前，桃樂絲把工作交付給同事。

199

Getting Married
結婚 🎧100

Cleo tells Felix about her uncertainty about marriage.
克莉歐將她對婚姻的遲疑告訴了菲力斯。

Felix: So are you really getting married tomorrow?

Cleo: Actually, I think I'm **getting cold feet**[1], but I could never tell that to my fiancé **face-to-face**[2].

Felix: Are you serious? What's happening? Come on, you have to **fill** me **in**[3]!

Cleo: Well, there's no question that I've really **fallen for**[4] him, but I'm just not sure that I want to **be with him**[5] forever.

Felix: I think that's perfectly normal. However, you're right—once you get married, it isn't as if you can **trade in**[6] one husband for another! **It figures**[7] that you would be nervous. I guess you really should think carefully about what you want.

fall for 愛上

菲力斯： 看來妳明天真的要結婚了？

克莉歐： 事實上，我有點**害怕**，但我不會把這件事情**當面**告訴我的未婚夫。

菲力斯： 妳是説真的嗎？怎麼了？説吧，**告訴**我吧！

克莉歐： 嗯，我真的非常**愛**他，但我不確定我是否想要和他**共度**一生。

菲力斯： 我想這很正常，不過妳説的沒錯，一旦結了婚，老公就不能**換**人了！妳會緊張是**理所當然**的。我想妳應該好好想想自己想要什麼。

get cold feet 害怕　　face-to-face 面對面　　fill in 告訴

101

1 get cold feet 緊張；害怕

- Ten minutes before the wedding, Francis **got cold feet** and ran off.
  婚禮前 10 分鐘，法蘭西斯太緊張所以臨陣脫逃了。

- You have always wanted to go bungee jumping, so don't **get cold feet** now!
  我知道你一直都想要嘗試高空彈跳，所以別緊張嘛！

- We're getting married next Saturday—that is, if Tom doesn't **get cold feet**!
  我們下星期天就要結婚了，假如湯姆沒有臨陣脫逃的話！

2 face-to-face 面對面

- Nate had spoken with Jeb a few times on the phone, but they had never met **face-to-face**.
  奈特和傑伯通過幾次電話，但他們從未見過面。

- I have a few friends whom I've never met **face-to-face** because we communicate online.
  我有幾個素未謀面的朋友，因為我們是在網路上認識的。

- She has refused a **face-to-face** interview, but she has agreed to answer my questions in a letter.
  她拒絕面對面會談，但同意在信中回覆我提到的問題。

3 fill (someone) in 告訴

- Anne **filled** the class **in** on her trip to Canada.
  安把加拿大之旅的事情告訴全班。

- After Clarence was **filled in** by Tyrone, the two guys got to work.
  泰倫告訴克萊倫斯該怎麼做後，兩人便開始行動。

- I **filled** him **in** on the latest gossip.
  我把最新的八卦告訴了他。

4 fall for 迷戀；被欺騙

- Poor Kim! She **fell for** a married man.
  可憐的金！她愛上了有婦之夫。

- Barry married the first woman he **fell for**.
  拜瑞和初戀女友結婚了。

- Our teacher **fell for** Dylan's story about being sick yesterday; actually, he was at the beach.
  狄倫騙老師說他昨天生病，其實他昨天去了海邊。

- I always **fall for** unsuitable men.
  我總是愛上了不該愛的男人。

- I stupidly **fell for** her story until someone told me she was already married.
  在別人告訴我她已婚之前，我一直傻傻相信她說的話。

- They met at a friend's party and **fell for** each other immediately.
  他們在朋友的派對上相遇，迅速地陷入熱戀。

- He told me he owned a castle in Spain, and I **fell for** it.
  他說他在西班牙擁有一座城堡，而我真的相信了。

5 be with (someone) 與某人談戀愛；了解某人說的話

- **Are** you **with** Patty, or are you still single?
  你和派蒂在交往嗎？還是你依然單身呢？

- You look puzzled—**are** you **with** me?
  你看起來很困惑，你了解我說的話嗎？

6 trade in （非金錢的）折抵；以物換物；以舊換新

- Erin got the price of the new car down when she offered to **trade in** her old SUV.
  艾琳新買的車子不貴，因為她用舊的 SUV 折抵。

- If I **trade in** this TV, will you lower the price of the new one? 如果我用這台電視來折抵，你願意算我便宜一點嗎？

102

7 it figures 理所當然

- **It figures** that it rained on my only day off of work this week.
  在我這星期唯一不用上班的這天，果然下雨了。

- **It figures** that you woke up late since you were at that party till 3 a.m. last night.
  你昨晚狂歡到半夜三點，今天當然會很晚起床。

8 be with it 得到訊息；快速理解

- Although my parents are not young people, they're really **with it**.
  雖然我的父母年紀不小，但他們真的懂很多。

- If you want to **be with it**, you'd better start paying more attention.
  如果你真的想要把它搞懂，最好專心一點。

- After a long night out, Jenna **wasn't** really **with it** at work the next day.
  珍娜昨晚在外面瘋了一整夜，隔天上班效率很差。

9 make (someone) tick 使做出某行為；賦予動機

- Lance is a strange guy; I really don't know what **makes** him **tick**.
  藍斯是個怪人，真不知道他為何要做出這些事情。

- I always wondered what **makes** the president **tick**.
  我一直在想總裁會如何應對。

10 cover for 撒謊掩護；暫時代替某人

- Please **cover for** Donna; she's sick this week.
  唐娜這星期請病假，請暫代她的職位。

- Although he knew his brother had eaten all the cookies, Dale **covered for** him.
  戴爾雖然知道弟弟吃了所有的餅乾，但還是幫他隱瞞。

11 give (someone) a break 饒了……；得了吧

- I know that Ruth is not doing her job well, but **give** her **a break**—it's her first day here!
  我知道茹絲的工作表現不理想，但饒了她吧，她才第一天上班！

- I know you're disappointed about your low test score, but **give** yourself **a break**. It was a very hard test, and no one did well!
  你的考試成績不好，我知道你很失望，但放過你自己吧，這次的考試很難，大家都考不好！

12 bow out 引退；退出

- Mark plans to **bow out** in six weeks, after having spent 20 years with the company.
  馬克在公司服務了 20 年之後，打算在六個星期後退休。

- After working as a senator for just a few months, Ms. Luther **bowed out** to accept a different job.
  在當了幾個月的參議員後，路瑟女士決定卸任，接受別份工作。

bow out 退出

I quit!

- An accident forced Jennifer to **bow out** of the show just before the first performance.
  一場意外讓珍妮佛在首演之前被迫退出。

The Missing iPod
失竊的 iPod  [103]

Gina and Mick talk about Dilbert.
吉娜和米克在談論呆伯特。

Mick: Do you know where Dilbert is?

Gina: **Search me**[1]! I haven't seen him for a few days.

Mick: Are you trying to **get a rise out of**[2] me? I just saw you speaking with him a few hours ago.

Gina: Okay, okay. Let me **get something off my chest**[3]. I'll be honest with you. I have seen Dilbert, but he doesn't want to talk to you.

Mick: But I have to talk to him. He's trying to **pin** the blame **on**[4] me for stealing his iPod—but I didn't do it.

Gina: I see. Fine, **stick around**[5] here, and I'll go get Dilbert. **By the way**[6], I don't think he'll **let** this **slide**[7] until he finds that MP3 player or someone pays for a new one.

Mick: I don't blame him, but there's no way I'll **pick up the tab**[8] for a new one. I didn't take it!

米克：　你知道呆伯特在哪嗎？

吉娜：　**不知道**！我好幾天沒看到他了。

米克：　妳想**惹火**我嗎？我幾個小時前才看到妳和他在聊天。

吉娜：　好吧，那我就**實話實說**了。老實說，我是有看到呆伯特，但他不想和你說話。

米克：　可是我有事情要告訴他。他想要把 iPod 被偷的事情**怪罪**到我身上來，但又不是我做的。

吉娜：　我知道了。好吧，在這裡**耐心等一下**，我去找呆伯特過來。噢，**對了**，在他找回 MP3，或有人買新的給他之前，我想他不會對這件事情**充耳不聞**的。

米克：　我不怪他，但我不會**付錢**買新的給他。又不是我偷的！

stick around 耐心等待　　　　　pick up the tab 付帳

207

104

1　search me　我不知道

- **Search me!** I have no idea where Fourth Avenue is.
  不知道！我完全不知道第四大道在哪裡。

2　get a rise out of　使生氣

- Arnold **got a rise out of** Gerald with his insulting comments.
  阿諾無禮的批評令傑拉爾德很生氣。

- Donny's teasing always **gets a rise out of** Mildred.
  唐尼的揶揄總是令米卓瑞德非常生氣。

3　get (something) off one's chest　把……傾吐出來；表明

- After Justin told Hailey his secret, he said it felt good to **get** it **off his chest**.
  賈斯汀把秘密告訴荷莉之後，他覺得說出來心情變好了許多。

- We listened as Brooke **got** her worries **off her chest**.
  我們在聽布洛克說她的困擾。

- I had spent six months worrying about it, and I was glad to **get** it **off my chest**.
  我已經為這件事情煩惱了六個月，很高興終於能夠把它說出來了。

4　pin on　怪罪……

- The police tried to **pin** the blame **on** Vanessa even though she wasn't there.
  雖然凡妮莎當時不在場，但警察還是企圖讓她背黑鍋。

- Gustavo **pinned** the crime **on** his neighbor.
  葛斯塔佛怪罪到鄰居身上。

208

5   stick around 耐心等待

- Please don't **stick around** here anymore; go home.
  請不要在這裡等了，回家去吧。

- Although they didn't have any money to spend, the teenagers **stuck around** the mall all day.
  這些年輕人即使沒有錢可花，但還是在購物中心待了一整天。

6   by the way 附帶一提

- It's nice meeting you; **by the way**, I'm Rick.
  很高興認識你，對了，我叫瑞克。

- It sure has been a busy day at the office! **By the way**, what are you doing this weekend?
  今天上班真的很忙，對了！你週末有什麼計畫嗎？

- I think we've discussed everything we need to. **By the way**, what time is it?
  我想所有需要討論的事情我們已經談完了。對了，現在幾點了？

7   let slide 丟下不管；忽視眼前的情況

- It's important to not **let** your responsibilities **slide**.
  千萬別忽視了你應負的責任。

- Alexis **let** her research paper **slide** and, in the end, never finished it.
  艾莉克絲忽略了她的研究報告，所以她最終沒有完成。

- I was doing really well with my diet, but I'm afraid I've **let** it **slide** recently.
  我的節食計畫原本進展得很順利，但恐怕我最近有點疏忽了。

- It's easy to **let** exercise **slide** when you feel bad, but that's when you need it the most.
  身體不舒服時最需要運動，但人們常會忽略這點。

105

8   pick up the tab 付帳

- Don't worry if you don't have any money. Andrea will **pick up the tab**.

  沒帶錢沒關係。安德麗雅會付錢的。

- Because I was the only one with a credit card, my friends asked me to **pick up the tab**. As usual, they didn't have enough money.

  朋友身上的錢一如往常地不夠，由於我是唯一擁有信用卡的人，所以朋友要我先付帳。

9   live it up   生活奢華

- Ella and Connor **lived it up** for a weekend in Las Vegas.

  艾拉和康諾在拉斯維加斯度過了一個奢華的週末。

- The couple **lived it up** during their honeymoon in Hawaii.

  這對夫妻到夏威夷度過了一個非常奢華的蜜月。

- She's alive and well and **living it up** in the Bahamas.

  她在巴哈馬的生活過得很好也很奢華。

10   liven up   使活躍

- The chef **livened up** the vanilla ice cream with fresh fruit and chocolate sauce.

  香草冰淇淋在新鮮水果和巧克力醬的裝飾下，變得非常可口動人。

- The meeting **livened up** when the CEO started telling some funny jokes.

  在執行長說了一些笑話後，這個會議變得活潑許多。

- A colored shirt can certainly **liven up** an outfit.

  色彩鮮明的襯衫絕對能夠讓穿著活了起來。

11　go to town 全心投入

- You can go out to eat anywhere you like, but don't **go to town** and spend all your money on one meal.
  你可以到任何你喜歡的餐廳吃飯，但別太投入而把所有的錢都花在一頓飯上面。

- Tom and Nicole have really **gone to town** on their wedding.
  湯姆和妮可全心全意地投入籌備婚禮。

go to town on the wedding
全心全意地投入籌備婚禮

12　have a voice in 擁有發言權

- In a true democracy, everyone **has a voice in** what the government does.
  在民主國家中，人民都擁有發言權。

- Whenever my company has an open position, the boss lets everyone **have a voice in** choosing the new employee.
  每當我們公司要聘請新員工時，老闆讓所有人都擁有選擇新同事的權利。

have a voice in
擁有發言權

Checking In

辦理住宿登記 🎧[106]

Joanne checks into a hotel.
瓊安在飯店登記住宿。

Clerk: Good evening, ma'am. Would you like to **check in**[1]?

Joanne: Yes, I would. Are there still nonsmoking rooms available?

Clerk: Don't worry. You haven't **missed the boat**[2]. There are plenty.

Joanne: That's good news; if there were no nonsmoking rooms here, I'm afraid I'd **lose my cool**[3]. My husband and I have been looking for a hotel all day! How much is one night here?

Clerk: A double room is $95 a night. I'll just need to see some ID.

Joanne: That's a great price. Oh, no! I think I left my ID with my husband. Can I show it to you later?

Clerk: No problem. I'll **take you at your word**[4] for now— but please remember to stop by with it later.

Joanne: Of course. I won't **cop out**[5].

Clerk: Here's your key. Remember you must **check out**[6] by 10:30 tomorrow morning.

Joanne: Is it possible to **leave open**[7] tomorrow night, too? We may stay two nights if this hotel **serves our purpose**[8].

Clerk: That's fine.

服務員：　晚安，女士。您要**辦理住宿登記**了嗎？

瓊安：　　是的。請問一下，禁菸樓層還有空房間嗎？

服務員：　別擔心，您並沒有**錯過**。我們還有許多空房間呢。

瓊安：　　太好了；若是沒有禁菸房間的話，我可能會**不知所措**。我和我先生整天都在找飯店投宿！請問住宿一晚的費用是多少錢？

服務員：　雙人房每晚是 95 元。我需要查看您的身分證。

瓊安：　　價錢很合理。噢，不會吧！我想我的身分證在我先生那裡我能夠等一下再給你看嗎？

服務員：　沒關係，我**相信**您，但稍後請務必拿過來。

瓊安：　　放心，我不會**逃避責任**的。

服務員：　這是您的鑰匙。請您記得明天早上 10 點 30 分前要**辦理退房**。

瓊安：　　我們可以明天晚上**才決定**嗎？如果這裡**符合**我們的需求，我們可能會待兩個晚上。

服務員：　好的。

1 check in 住房登記

- Before you can stay at this hotel, it is necessary to **check in** at the front desk.
  入住飯店前，要先到櫃檯辦理住宿登記。

- Is it possible to **check in** at the hotel after midnight?
  我可以在半夜登記住宿嗎？

2 miss the boat 錯過機會

- We could have bought cheap tickets to L.A. yesterday, but we **missed the boat** by thinking about it too much, and now they're all gone.
  我們昨天本來可以買到飛往洛杉磯的便宜機票，但我們因為考慮了太多而錯失機會，票現在都賣完了。

- This is your last chance to accept this job; if you are still unsure, I'm afraid you'll have **missed the boat**.
  這是你最後接受這份工作的機會，如果你還是無法決定，恐怕會錯過機會。

3 lose one's cool 失去冷靜；情緒激動；沉不住氣

- When Aaron heard that he had failed the class, he **lost his cool** and started crying like a child.
  亞倫知道他這科的成績不及格後，情緒很激動，接著哭得像個孩子。

- I know that Felix is an annoying guy, but don't **lose your cool** if he upsets you; just stay calm.
  我知道菲力斯是個很討厭的人，但當他惹你不高興時，不要激動，要保持冷靜。

4 take one at one's word 相信某人說的話

- Although Aiden didn't have a written agreement, he **took his boss at his word** and started working the next day.

  雖然艾登沒有接到書面通知，但他相信老闆說的話，並且隔天就開始上班。

- Joel is an honest guy. You can definitely **take him at his word**.

  喬爾絕對是個老實人，你可以完全相信他說的話。

5 cop out 逃避責任

- Go talk to that pretty girl; don't **cop out** now!

  去和那個漂亮女孩說話吧，別再逃避了！

- Just as the group was about to go mountain climbing, Diane **copped out** and said she was too nervous.

  就在登山隊準備出發時，黛安因為太緊張，所以放棄了。

- Martin **copped out** of the parachute jump at the last minute with some feeble excuse.

  馬汀在最後一刻因為一些牽強的理由而放棄了跳傘。

6 check out 辦理退房；結帳離開；檢查；看看

- Be sure to **check out** before noon tomorrow.

  明天中午前一定要辦理退房。

- If you have time today, could you please **check out** the weather forecast for this week?

  你今天有時間的話，可以請你查一下這週的天氣預報嗎？

check out 辦理退房

- I'm going to **check out** that new club.
  我要去看看那家新開的俱樂部。

- I **checked** three books **out** of the library this afternoon.
  我今天下午向圖書館借了三本書。

7   leave open   暫緩決定

- Danielle **left open** the possibility that she could drive me to school, but she said she wasn't sure yet.
  丹妮葉拉暫時還沒決定是否要載我去學校，她還不確定。

- Brenda **left** the weekend **open** just in case her boyfriend invited her to the party.
  布蘭達暫緩決定週末計畫，免得男朋友邀請她參加派對。

8   serve (the/one's) purpose   符合需求

- Before you spend a lot of money on those programs, you should be sure they will **serve your purpose**.
  你在投入資金前，應該要先確定這些案子是否符合你的需求。

- This new laptop will surely **serve the purpose**.
  這台新的筆記型電腦肯定能符合我的需求。

9   line up   排隊；安排

- The security guards made us **line up** to get into the club.
  安全人員要我們排隊進入俱樂部。

- The little boy **lined up** all his toy cars so he could see each one.
  小男孩把所有的玩具車都排成一列，以便他看到每台車。

line up 排隊

10　turn on
由……決定；持敵對的態度；使高興

- Your grade in this class **turns on** how well you do on the final paper.
  你的期末報告決定了你在班上的成績。

- The dog **turned on** Lola and tried to bite her.
  那隻狗對蘿娜產生敵意，而且還企圖咬她。

- Suddenly, Vicky just **turned on** me and accused me of undermining her.
  維琪突然對我產生敵意並且指責我暗中說她壞話。

11　in the worst way
渴望地；緊急地；非常

- Jasmine wants to live in Texas **in the worst way**.
  賈思敏非常想要住在德州。

- Phil wanted to buy that video game **in the worst way**, but he didn't have enough cash.
  菲爾非常想要買那台電動玩具，但他的錢不夠。

- After a day in the hot sun, I needed a shower **in the worst way**.
  在大太陽底下待了一天，我非常地想要沖澡。

12　think up
突發奇想；捏造

- Harriet **thought up** a great topic for her thesis.
  哈莉特突然想到一個很棒的論文主題。

- Paul **thought up** his own chicken soup recipe.
  保羅想出了獨家的雞湯食譜。

- I don't want to go tonight, but I can't **think up** a good excuse.
  我今晚不想去，但我想不到好的理由拒絕。

Showing Off
炫燿賣弄 🎧109

Bob shows Angie his new mobile phone.
鮑伯把新手機拿給安姬看。

Bob: Take a look at my new cell phone! It is also a camera and an MP3 player, and it can even go online. It can also do a lot of other cool stuff, but I'm still **learning the ropes**[1].

Angie: Hmm . . . that's interesting. When someone calls you, does it have a special ring?

Bob: That's the best part! Whenever I get a call, it makes the sound of a cow. That's sure to **make waves**[2].

Angie: I'm sure. You know, it is a cool phone, but you shouldn't **show off**[3] so much. Where did you buy it, anyway?

Bob: This phone **was up for grabs**[4] in a hot dog-eating competition, and I won! Those competitions are a great way to win prizes. There's another one next month, and the winner gets a flat screen TV. You want to compete, too?

Angie: No way, man. **Not on your life**[5]!

Bob: Okay. Well, **keep your fingers crossed**[6] for me.

鮑伯： 妳看我的新手機！它也是相機、MP3 播放器，還可以上網。我想它還有許多很新的功能，但我還在**摸索**當中。

安姬： 嗯，聽起來不錯。那有人打電話給你時，有什麼特別的鈴聲嗎？

鮑伯： 這就是這支手機最棒的地方！只要有人打電話給我，手機就會發出牛叫聲。許多人肯定會**非常驚訝**。

安姬： 我也覺得。這支手機很棒，但你不應該到處**炫燿**。總之，你在哪裡買的呢？

鮑伯： **每位**參加吃熱狗大賽的人**都有機會贏得**這支手機，所以手機是我贏來的！參加比賽是贏得獎品很好的方式。下個月還有一場比賽，贏的人可以得到液晶電視。妳也想參加比賽嗎？

安姬： 才沒有。**想都別想！**

鮑伯： 好吧。那就為我**祈禱**吧。

show off 炫耀

keep one's fingers crossed 祈求

219

110

1   learn the ropes 摸索

- It's my first day working here, so I still need to **learn the ropes**.
  今天是我第一天上班，所以我還在摸索當中。

- No one will expect you to do much around the office until you are trained and have **learned the ropes**.
  在你完成培訓並抓到要領前，公司是不會派給你太多任務的。

- It'll take time for the new receptionist to **learn the ropes**.
  新來的接待員要花一些時間來摸索工作內容。

2   make waves 引起眾人議論；引起抱怨

- Pam got fired from her job because she was always **making waves** during important meetings.
  潘老是在重要會議中挑起事端，所以她被解雇了。

- The key to working well with a team is to not **make** too many **waves**.
  團隊合作的關鍵就是不要興風作浪。

- Our culture encourages us to fit the norm and avoid **making waves**.
  我們的文化鼓勵我們行為舉止要合乎規範，不要興風作浪。

3   show off 炫耀

- Don can be really annoying. Whenever there are pretty girls around, he always tries to **show off** his physical strength.
  唐有時很討人厭，只要有漂亮女生在旁邊，他總會想要炫耀他那壯碩的身材。

- I think Melissa could be a good basketball player if she stopped **showing off** and was more of a team player.
  只要梅麗莎別再炫耀，多點團隊精神，我認為她會成為一名優秀的籃球員。

4 be up for grabs 讓他人也能得到或贏得

- The new car **is up for grabs** in the marathon!
  贏得馬拉松比賽的人可以得到這台新車！

- The math teacher's job **is up for grabs** because he's quitting.
  他要辭職了，所以數學老師一職空了出來。

5 not on your life 別妄想

- You think I'll let you go to New York by yourself? **Not on your life**!
  你以為我會讓你獨自去紐約嗎？想都別想！

6 keep one's fingers crossed 祈求

- Your little sister has a big test today, so **keep your fingers crossed** for her.
  你妹妹今天有重要考試，所以為她祈禱吧。

- **Keep your fingers crossed**! I have a job interview this afternoon.
  我今天下午有工作面談，替我祈禱吧！

7 carry on 驚慌失措；繼續

- The little kids **carried on** all night because they had eaten too much candy.
  孩子們整個晚上吵個不停，因為他們吃了太多的糖果了。

- As soon as the movie was over, Caroline **carried on** with her homework.
  電影一演完，卡若琳便繼續做功課。

111

8 cover ground 涉及的範圍

- The big research project is due soon, so we tried to **cover** a lot of **ground** before Monday.
  這份報告再不久就要送出，我們必須趕在星期一之前完成所有的細節。

- The students **covered ground** on all the issues during their discussion. 學生的討論涉及了所有的議題。

9 mind the store 負責看守

- While Mr. Richardson was away from the office, Jack **minded the store**.
  理查森先生不在辦公室時，是由傑克暫時打理一切。

- Who's going to be **minding the store** while your manager's away?
  經理不在時，是由誰負責管理的？

10 throw the book at (someone) 嚴厲懲罰

- When Julia was first caught by the police officers, they didn't punish her too much; the second time, however, they **threw the book at** her.
  警察第一次抓到茱莉亞時，並沒有很嚴厲地懲罰她。然而他們第二次抓到她時，便對她施以嚴懲。

- After several arrests for drunken driving, the judge finally **threw the book at** Jack.
  傑克好幾次被抓到酒醉駕車，法官終於對他做出嚴厲的判決。

11 throw (someone) a curve

提出意想不到的事情（通常含有負面意思）

- Victoria's dad really **threw** her **a curve** when he said she couldn't do anything special for her birthday— the fact was, he had planned a surprise party.

  維多莉亞的爸爸騙她沒有準備特別的生日計畫。事實上，他策劃了一場驚喜派對。

- Lisa **threw** me **a curve** by asking me to go to the theater instead of the mall.

  莉莎意想不到地約我去看電影，而不是去逛街。

- Jerry really **threw** me **a curve** when he asked me a personal question at work.

  傑瑞上班時問了一個令我意想不到的私人問題。

12 put one's foot in it

搞砸；說錯話

- I really **put my foot in it** yesterday when the boss overheard me making fun of her.

  老闆昨天無意中聽到我在開她玩笑，我想我真的搞砸了。

- I really **put my foot in it** with Diane. I didn't realize she was a vegetarian.

  我真的搞砸了與黛安之間的關係。我並不知道她吃素。

The First Week at College
大學生活的第一個星期 🎧112

Samantha talks to Al about her first week at college.
莎曼莎跟艾爾說起她第一個星期的大學生活。

Al:	How was your first week at college?
Samantha:	Well, it was hard! In the beginning, I felt like I **was over my head**[1].
Al:	Why do you say that?
Samantha:	I needed help all the time. Luckily, I had the best tutor a student could **ask for**[2], but I knew things weren't supposed to be that tough.
Al:	So what happened?
Samantha:	I had to **take the bull by the horns**[3] and really study harder. College **is a far cry from**[4] high school, and although my professors are happy to **give me a hand**[5] sometimes, I had to learn how to be a better student.
Al:	So now you can deal with what your professors **dish out**[6]?
Samantha:	**By all means**[7]! There's no doubt.
Al:	It sure sounds like you **landed on your feet**[8] after those early difficulties. Congratulations!

艾爾： 妳在大學的第一個星期過得如何呢？

莎曼莎： 唉，很難熬！我一開學就**忙得一個頭兩個大**。

艾爾： 怎麼說？

莎曼莎： 我總是需要別人的幫助。幸好我有一位可以**求助**的好助教，可是我覺得事情應該沒那麼困難才對。

艾爾： 發生了什麼事情嗎？

莎曼莎： 我得**不畏艱難**，並且更用功唸書；大學**和**高中**不同**，雖然有時教授很樂意**幫助**我，但我必須要學會如何成為好學生。

艾爾： 所以妳現在能夠應付教授**指派**的作業了嗎？

莎曼莎： **那當然**！別懷疑。

艾爾： 看來妳已經從之前所遇到的困難中，**重新振作起來**了。恭喜妳！

give sb. a hand 幫助

land on one's feet 重新振作起來

113

1   be over one's head   太難以致無法理解

- Jonny is pretty young, so a lot of the jokes that the older boys were telling **were over his head**.
  強尼年紀很輕，那些較年長的男孩所開的玩笑，超出了他所能理解的範圍。

- Everything Aiden heard in the class was really interesting, but a lot of it **was over his head**.
  艾登在課堂上所學到的東西都很有趣，但有些超出他所能理解的範圍。

- The math homework was really tough. It **was** way **over my head**.
  數學作業真的很難，這已經遠超出我所能理解的範圍了。

2   ask for   自討苦吃；應得；要求

- You are **asking for** it if you don't clean up your room like Mom ordered.
  如果你不照媽媽要求打掃房間，就是自討苦吃了。

- Dr. O'Maley is the best dentist anyone could **ask for**; he's professional, friendly, and kind.
  歐邁利醫生是最優秀的牙醫，每個人都想給他看診。他很專業、友善和親切。

3   take the bull by the horns   不畏艱難

- Roland didn't want Alison at his party, but he was too shy to **take the bull by the horns** and tell her to leave.
  羅蘭不想要艾莉森參加他的派對，但他太膽小而不敢開口要她離開。

- If you are unhappy with your life, it may be time to **take the bull by the horns** and try something new.
  如果你對生活不滿意，應該要嘗試新事物。

226

4 be a far cry from 與……相差甚遠

- New York **is** really **a far cry from** the little village where I was born.

  紐約和我所出生的小村落真的有很大的差異。

- This little stream **is a far cry from** the Mississippi River.

  這條小溪和密西西比河相比，簡直就是天壤之別。

5 give (someone) a hand 幫助

- Will someone please **give** me **a hand** moving these boxes?

  有人可以幫我搬這些箱子嗎？

- Ivan **gave** Muriel **a hand** with her work because she needed help.

  穆芮需要幫忙，艾文便幫她做功課。

6 dish out 脫口而出；分發

- Mira was in a great mood, and she **dished out** compliments to everyone she saw.

  米拉心情很好，她不假思索地稱讚每個她見到的人。

- The waiter **dished out** soup to everyone at our table.

  服務生送湯給在座的每個人。

7 by all means 一定；當然；不用說

- **By all means**, feel free to use my apartment when I'm on vacation.

  我去度假時，你當然可以隨意使用我的公寓。

- Well, there's still an extra seat available in the car, so come along with us, **by all means**.

  嗯，車子還有空位，你當然可以和我們坐同台車。

- "May I borrow this pen?" "**By all means**."

  「可以借我這隻原子筆嗎？」「當然。」

227

114

8 land on one's feet 安然脫險；重新振作起來

- No matter what crazy things happen to Tiffany, she always **lands on her feet**; she's a very smart woman.
  無論蒂芬妮遇到什麼事情，她總是能夠安然脫險；她是一個很聰明的女人。

- Bobby really **landed on his feet** with that raise at work.
  巴比靠著工作加薪而重新振作起來。

- It may take a few months to get a job, but I'm sure you'll **land on your feet**.
  找工作可能會花上好幾個月，但我相信你一定會重新振作起來的。

9 get through to (someone) 使了解；聯絡上

- Despite the best efforts of Jeff's friends and family, no one could **get through to** him and convince him to stay in college.
  除了傑夫的朋友和家人，沒有人能夠與傑夫溝通，並且說服他繼續就學。

- Barney finally **got through to** his girlfriend about exercising more.
  巴尼終於讓女朋友了解到她必須多運動了。

- I **got through to** the wrong department.
  我聯絡錯部門了。

- We can't **get through to** the government just how serious the problem is!
  我們無法讓政府理解問題的嚴重性！

- Pictures can sometimes help you **get through to** people more effectively than writing can.
  圖片有時候比文字更容易幫助人們理解。

10 get out from under 解決債務；擺脫負擔

- Ron wasn't sure how to **get out from under** his credit card debt, so he started looking for a second job.
朗不知道要如何解決卡債，所以他開始找兼職工作。

11 keep one's word 遵守約定；值得信任

- You can really count on Dan—he's the kind of guy who **keeps his word**.
你可以相信丹，他是個說話算話的人。

- I hope I can trust you to **keep your word**.
我希望你能夠遵守約定。

- I said I'd visit him, and I shall **keep my word**.
我說過會去拜訪他，而我應該遵守約定。

- Jeff is someone who **keeps his word**—you can rely on that.
傑夫是個說話算話的人，很可靠。

My Note

Getting Home Late
晚回家 🎧115

Ernie calls his mom to tell her he got in trouble
at school and will be home late.
爾尼打電話告訴媽媽他在學校惹上麻煩，所以會晚點回家。

Ernie: Hi, Mom? I won't **be in**[1] until late today. I have to stay after school.

Mom: Why? What did you do?

Ernie: It was all Ms. Butterworth's fault. She's the one who is making me stay late.

Mom: Were you **goofing off**[2]?

Ernie: Well, yeah, a little. Also, when Ms. Butterworth asked where my report was, I **talked back to**[3] her.

Mom: Why did you do that?

Ernie: She was **keeping after**[4] me to finish my report . . . I was in a bad mood.

Mom: I guess that's where she **drew the line**[5]. Anyway, if I **were in her shoes**[6], I'd probably do the same thing. You were really **getting out of line**[7].

Ernie: Can I still go to the dance this weekend?

Mom: Hmm, I'm not sure. Let's **play it by ear**[8].

Ernie: Oh Mom!

爾尼： 嗨，老媽？我今天會晚點**回家**。我放學後必須留下來。

媽媽： 為什麼？你做了什麼好事？

爾尼： 都是巴特沃斯老師的錯，是她要我留那麼晚的。

媽媽： 你又**偷懶**了嗎？

爾尼： 嗯，算是吧。還有，巴特沃斯女士問我報告交了沒時，我和她**頂嘴**。

媽媽： 你為何要那麼做？

爾尼： 她一直**嘮嘮叨叨**要我寫完報告……而我當時心情不太好。

媽媽： 我想這就是她**無法接受**的原因了。總之，如果我**是她**的話，我可能也會這麼做。你真是太**沒規矩**了。

爾尼： 那我這星期還可以去參加舞會嗎？

媽媽： 嗯，我還不確定。**要看你的表現**囉。

爾尼： 噢，老媽！

231

1 be in 在家；在公司；流行

- What time will you **be in** tomorrow?
  你明天幾點會在家？

- I'm sorry, but the doctor **is** not **in** today.
  很抱歉，醫生今天休診。

- I heard that colorful sandals **are in** this summer.
  我聽說今年流行顏色鮮豔的涼鞋。

2 goof off 摸魚；偷懶

- Jan **goofed off** last weekend and went camping when she should have been painting the house.
  珍上週末本來應該要油漆房子，但她偷懶跑去露營。

- The reason you're getting a bad grade in this class is because you **goofed off** when you should have been doing your homework.
  該做功課時，你卻在摸魚，這就是你在班上成績不好的原因。

3 talk back to 頂嘴；說話無禮

- Grandpa was mad when my little sister **talked back to** him.
  爺爺對我妹妹和他頂嘴感到很生氣。

- Don't you ever **talk back to** me again! 你還敢頂嘴！

4 keep after 不斷詢問；嘮嘮叨叨

- The teacher **kept after** Art until he finished his report.
  老師一直嘮嘮叨叨直到亞特寫完報告。

- I **kept after** Lucas to let me borrow his car for the weekend, and in the end, he agreed.
  我一直問盧卡斯週末是否可以把車借給我，他最後終於同意了。

5　draw the line　堅持不做某事；區別

- Although Phil sometimes has a piece of chocolate or two, he **draws the line** at cake because he is trying to lose weight.
  雖然菲爾有時會吃一、兩塊巧克力，但他為了減肥拒吃蛋糕。

- My parents told me I have to be home by midnight; although they don't mind if I'm a little late, they **draw the line** at 12:30.
  我父母要我在午夜前回家，雖然我覺得晚點到家無所謂，但他們堅持不超過 12 點 30 分。

6　be in (someone's) shoes　站在某人的立場

- Oh, boy! I wouldn't like to **be in** your **shoes** when you tell your dad that you locked the keys in the car!
  噢，天啊！如果我是你，就不會把你是如何把鑰匙留在車內的事情告訴你爸！

- What would you do if you **were in** my **shoes**?
  如果你是我的話，會怎麼做呢？

7　get out of line　不守規矩

- Please behave when we visit my aunt and don't **get out of line**.
  到我阿姨家拜訪時，要注意你的行為舉止，不可以不守規矩。

- The teacher told Amanda that if she **gets out of line** one more time, he'll have to kick her out of class.
  老師告訴亞曼達要是再不守規矩，他就只好把她趕出教室了。

8 play (something) by ear
憑印象演奏；
隨機應變；見機行事

- For now, John is a math major in college. He has decided to **play** it **by ear** as to whether he'll get a degree in physics instead.
約翰目前主修數學，他不確定他之後是否能夠轉系，而他現在決定要見機行事看能否取得物理學位。

- I'm not sure if we'll go to the park this weekend; let's **play** it **by ear**.
我不確定這週末是否要去公園；看情況吧。

- Maggie can **play** anything on the piano **by ear**.
瑪姬只要聽過一遍旋律，便可以用鋼琴彈奏出來。

9 fix up
修理；安排

- The teenagers spent the weekend **fixing up** the old truck. By Sunday night, it was working like new!
一群年輕人利用週末修理卡車，他們在星期日傍晚前就讓卡車變得像新的一樣！

fix up 修理

234

10 dry run 排練；預演

- Although Sandra thought she had practiced playing the flute enough, she made some mistakes during the **dry run** and realized that she needed to practice a lot more before the performance.
  雖然珊卓拉認為她的笛子已經吹得非常熟練，但她在排練時犯了一些錯，她覺得在表演前需要再多練習一下。

- In the weeks before he went onstage with his monologue, Brian did a **dry run** every night.
  在演出的好幾個星期前，布萊恩每天晚上都在為獨角戲排練。

- They decided to do a **dry run** at the church the day before the wedding.
  他們決定婚禮前在教堂做一次預演。

11 be had 被騙

- When you go shopping for a new computer, it's a good idea to bring along an expert so you don't end up **being had**.
  買新電腦時，最好找一位內行人陪你去，才不會被騙。

- I'm sorry to tell you this, but if you just spent $1,200 on this stereo, you **were had**.
  很遺憾地告訴你，如果你花了 1,200 元買了這個音響，你肯定被騙了。

- If you paid much for this car, you've **been had**!
  如果這台車花了你很多錢，那你肯定是被騙了！

LEARN SMART!
狄克生片語 這樣背

作 者	Matt Coler
審 訂	Judy M. Majewsky
翻 譯	李盈瑩

編 輯	丁宥暄
內 文 排 版	林書玉／執筆者企業社
封 面 設 計	林書玉
製 程 管 理	洪巧玲
出 版 者	寂天文化事業股份有限公司
電 話	02-2365-9739
傳 真	02-2365-9835
網 址	www.icosmos.com.tw
讀 者 服 務	onlineservice@icosmos.com.tw

出 版 日 期	2020 年 1 月	初版二刷	320101
郵 撥 帳 號	1998620-0　寂天文化事業股份有限公司		

- 訂購金額 600（含）元以上免郵資處理費
- 訂購金額 600 元以下，需外加 65 元郵資處理費。

【若有破損，請寄回更換，謝謝。】

國家圖書館出版品預行編目資料

Learn Smart! 狄克生片語這樣背 / Matt Coler 作. --
初版 . --【臺北市】：寂天文化, 2020.01

面；公分.

背誦版
ISBN 978-986-318-414-0（25K 平裝附光碟片）
ISBN 978-986-318-881-0（32K 平裝附光碟片）

1. 英語　2. 慣用語

805.123　　　　　　　　　　　108022476